Craving You
Dani Rose

Copyright © 2025 by Emily Klepp

All rights reserved.

No part of this publication may be reproduced, distributed, or transmitted in any form or by any means, including photocopying, recording, or other electronic or mechanical methods, without the prior written permission of the publisher, except as permitted by U.S. copyright law. For permission requests, contact emilyklepp@edknovels.com.

The story, all names, characters, and incidents portrayed in this production are fictitious. No identification with actual persons (living or deceased), places, buildings, and products is intended or should be inferred.

Book Cover by Emily Klepp

Edited and Formatted by: Jade Katzchen

Edited by Becky from In the Mind of a Smut Services

1st edition 2025

Contents

Dedication	V
Craving You	VI
Your Mental Health Matters	VII
Chapter One	1
Chapter Two	13
Chapter Three	23
Chapter Four	36
Chapter Five	42
Chapter Six	52
Chapter Seven	58
Chapter Eight	67
Chapter Nine	74
Chapter Ten	102
Chapter Eleven	118
Chapter Twelve	127

Chapter Thirteen	146
Chapter Fourteen	154
Chapter Fifteen	157
Chapter Sixteen	180
Chapter Seventeen	188
Chapter Eighteen	191
Chapter Nineteen	203
Chapter Twenty	229
Chapter Twenty-One	246
Chapter Twenty-Two	256
Chapter Twenty-Three	263
Chapter Twenty-Four	273
Chapter Twenty-Five	285
Chapter Twenty-Six	294
Epilogue	299
About the author	303
How to contact the author	304

Dedicated to the ones who find their new kinks in the books they read...

This is not the one, baby.

It's red flag city up in this bitch.

Craving You

These men will crave you, take you, and break you. It's more than a simple obsession; our souls beg to be connected. No matter how much I fight it, I can't resist them when I'm asleep. Why does something so forbidden feel so right?

These men... They'll be the death of me.

Your Mental Health Matters

This is a dark romance book with <u>**HEAVY**</u> triggers. Reader's discretion is <u>**HIGHLY**</u> advised... Please don't ignore my warning!

For a full list of TW and tropes, visit edknovels.com

Your mental health matters

<u>**National Domestic Violence Hotline**</u>

1-800-799-7233

<u>**National Sexual Assault Hotline**</u>

1-800-656-4673

<u>**Suicide and Crisis Lifeline**</u>

988

Help IS available.

Chapter One
Lorelei

THE MUSIC IS PULSING through my body as I wrap my hand around the smooth pole. The lights are dim throughout the club, but all the spotlights are on me. I hook my leg around the pole before gracefully twirling around. I have trained for years to be able to get myself upside down so I can effortlessly work my body up the pole so I can lock my ankles around it. Once I feel secure, my hands are free. The crowd hollers and gets rowdy when I unhook my already transparent lace bra and let it drop to the ground. I grab a tight hold on the pole before flipping myself off and landing on the stage in a split, making my breasts bounce and jiggle from the drop. I sway to the beat as I drag my hands down my body to draw attention to every curve. I smoothly turn myself around so I can grab hold of the pole once more to stand myself up. I go slow and make a point to stick my ass out. I have a thong on that hardly covers anything, but it's the bare minimum for the law. Which is humorous considering I get railed in the back room by billionaire executives for extra money.

"Give it up for the lovely Miss Lolita," the DJ says as I blow the crowd a seductive kiss and strut off stage. The moment I am behind the curtain, I roll my eyes and flop down in a chair to wait for the bouncer to bring me the cash off the stage. Omar is the one on tonight. I like Omar. He works every Friday and Saturday when I am here and always stays close when I am in the back rooms. Sometimes we have clients who get a little too rough, and he keeps us safe.

"Hey, pretty girl," Omar says as he hands me my stack of cash.

"Hey," I say. "Thanks."

"You are making good money tonight," he remarks as I stand. "You still going to the back?"

"How else am I going to get fucked, Omar?" I ask.

"Baby girl, you say the word and I'll bend your sexy ass over," he winks.

"Omar, honey. You are gay," I laugh. "Yes. I have one of my regulars tonight, so I'll just be back there for him."

"I don't like you back there, Lorelei," he says with a frown. I tuck my money away in my little bag before we walk on the main floor. He stays close so no one can stop me. Once in the back hall, I stop walking and grab a thin robe from the hook and put it on. It hardly covers my ass, and my tits are still mostly out.

"I'll stop eventually," I say. "I take one client a night, and I'm only here two days a week since I started working for my brother."

"Girl, what if he comes in here?" he asks. "Or his friend?"

"Cam and Remy would never come in here, first of all. Second, Cam knows that I used to dance. He would just think I needed to be paid more and try to give me a raise."

"Girl, you make good fucking money working for him. Why?"

"Dancing is my escape," I shrug. "My regular tonight might have brought someone with him, so stay close. Usually, the friends are the ones who cause trouble."

"Girl, bye. Be safe and cut his dick off if he doesn't wear a rubber," he says with a sigh. I go up on my tiptoes and kiss his cheek before going down the hall into the last room.

When I enter, three men look up at me from the couch. Shit. I hate when there are more than two. I am going to be sore all weekend. "Evening, boys," I say sweetly.

"Lolita," one of the men says with a smirk. He is the one I usually see. I refuse to tell him my name, so I don't know his. He comes in weekly and fucks me and has since my first weekend here four years ago. I usually just call him sir, because I have no idea what else to call him.

When I get close, he pulls me to stand between his legs and runs his hands up my thighs. I giggle when he smacks my ass with both hands and squeezes my cheeks. "Good evening, sir," I say as I climb into his lap to straddle him. He unties my robe before slowly taking it off. When it falls to the ground, he takes one of my nipples into his mouth and sucks. I sigh and close my eyes. I let my head fall back as his other hand comes up and gently pinches and tugs at my other nipple.

"Ready for some fun?" he asks.

"I'm always ready for whatever you have in store for me," I say with another smile as I rock my hips against his. He groans, and I do it again.

"On your knees, Lolita. Show the boys how perfect your mouth is," he says. I move out of his lap and sink to the floor on my knees between his legs. He sits back and watches me as I slowly pull his cock free.

I start by licking up the backside of his cock before swirling my tongue around the head. I then take him straight down my throat and suck hard. He fists my hair and pushes me down until I gag before letting me move again. He is more aggressive tonight than usual, but he always is when he brings friends. I have never seen these guys before, though.

"You gonna play with the whore, or are you gonna show us what she can do?" one of the men asks. Sir chuckles before standing. I am in no position to fight back now, so I open my mouth again when he grabs my head with a tight grip. He shoves back down my throat before he starts violently fucking it. I immediately start hitting his leg, trying to tell him to back off, but another man pulls my arms behind my back.

"That's it. Choke on it, Lolita," Sir groans. I have tears rolling down my cheeks as I try not to panic. I can't exactly call for Omar with a cock in my mouth, so I just do my best to stop fighting. Once they all get off, they'll leave anyhow. My fear is what the other two will do if they antagonize Sir into being this violent with me. He has never been this forceful. If I tap him, he has always at least slowed down. When Sir finally comes, one of the others pinches my nose closed and forces me to swallow before he pulls out of my mouth.

I fall down to my hands, coughing and gasping for air, but one of the other men grabs me by the hair and drags me back up. His cock is already out, and he has a condom on, so I cooperate when he pulls me into his lap. Usually, Sir works with me to make sure I am ready to take him, but this fucker simply covers my mouth and slams into me. I scream against his hand as pain shoots through me. The other man wastes no time spreading my ass cheeks and spitting on me before shoving the full length of his dick deep inside of me. I can tell he has a condom on too, but they are so minimally lubricated that when they both start to fuck me hard and fast, the friction brings a constant stream of screams out of me that are well muffled by the hand over my mouth.

"Fuuuck, this bitch is tight," the man in my ass groans.

I am nearly sobbing as they fuck me as hard as they can. My belly hurts so badly; I just want this to end already. Maybe Omar is right, and I need to stop doing this. This thought is solidified when my crying bothers the man under me. Out of nowhere, he uncovers my mouth and slaps me so hard that I see stars. I am completely dazed as they finish, and I am dumped on the ottoman. I am staring up at the ceiling as I hear them take off their condoms.

"We'll come see you tomorrow," Sir says softly as he leans down and kisses my forehead. He puts a wad of cash in my hand before simply walking out.

What the fuck just happened? He really knocked the shit out of me. Why? I sit myself up, and I am still dizzy as I find my robe and put it back on. My thong was basically torn off me earlier, so I finish taking it off and throw it away.

I hear Omar behind me, but I am still so out of it that I don't respond. "Lorelei, look at me," Omar says firmly as he grabs my shoulders and turns me around. "Rob!"

"He hit me," I say.

"Yeah, I can see that," he says as he scoops me into his arms and carries me out. Instead of taking me through the main floor, he takes me down a back hall to go around to the other side of the building.

"What happened?" Rob, my boss, says from behind us.

"The last client knocked the shit out of her," Omar says. "She's done going back there. I don't care if I have to burn this fucking building down. She's done."

He sets me down in a chair before pulling another one up to sit in front of me. "He said they were coming back tomorrow," I say.

"They?" Rob asks, lifting my chin to look at my face. "Jesus, he really smacked the shit out of you, girl."

"There were three," I say, still dazed.

"Only George was supposed to be in there," Rob says. "I'll pull the footage."

"I don't wanna go back there anymore, Rob," I say.

"Okay," he says softly. "Lorelei, I'm sorry this happened. He's never been like that with you before."

"It wasn't him. It was the guys he brought. It's like he was showing me off," I say. "I don't want to dance tomorrow, though."

"Okay. I'm going to take you off for a few weeks and we can talk after," he says.

"Is that your way of telling me to quit?" I ask.

"Yes," Rob says. "I'm also banning George."

"That's his name?" I ask. "He's never told me before because I wouldn't tell him my real name."

"Weird... Yeah. I'm banning him. I'll check the cameras to see who the others were."

"I'm going to go home, if that's okay," I say.

"You gonna be okay getting home?" Rob asks.

"Yeah," I sigh. "I'm okay. Just needed a second. I don't know why he hit me. Then George just handed me a wad of cash like it was nothing."

"How much?" Omar asks.

"Hell, I don't know. I'll count when I get home," I say. Omar hands me my little bag that I keep my money in, and I put the rest of my cash in before I stand.

"Lorelei," Omar says.

"I know," I say. "I'm just used to being here."

"Dance, but don't go into the back rooms anymore. No private dances," Rob says. "You've been here for a while, and a lot of the regulars recognize you, which always leads to them being rougher with you because they assume you will take it."

"The new ones are the ones who will take it," I say.

"Most girls don't stay in a club more than a year, and you've been here four," Rob says. "Consider switching clubs or stopping. You have a master's degree, babe. You don't need to be here. You can pay and take classes on the weekends."

"I'll think about it," I say.

"Want me to walk you out?" Omar asks.

"Nah. You have girls to watch over," I say. "I'm walking back to the apartment anyhow."

"Why not get a cab?" Rob asks. "I can get you one."

"You paying? That shit is expensive," I frown.

"I'll pay if you aren't walking home," he says. "Go get dressed."

I GET OUT OF the cab and lazily walk into my apartment building. I just want to drink some hot tea and go to sleep. When I get into the elevator, I lay my head back and close my eyes. I almost forget there is someone in here with me. He isn't paying attention, though. He has his hood up, headphones in, and head down. I think he lives in the building because I see him fairly often in passing. Although, I have no idea what he looks like.

I open my eyes, and his head snaps back so that I don't see him. Aww. He's shy. The elevator door opens for my floor. "Have a good night," I say as I step out. I walk down the hall to my apartment, thinking about my bed. I am so ready to go to sleep, but I want to shower first.

When I get in, I start stripping off my clothes and toss them all in the hamper before turning the shower on. I go through my usual routine of setting the kettle on the stove to heat water while I shower. When I get back to the bathroom, I stop and look at myself in the mirror.

I am five feet one inch tall with long, wavy auburn hair and green eyes. I have a perfectly rounded ass, thick thighs, wide hips, a curved waist, and large breasts. I am pretty, but that's all people see me as. They don't see the master's degree in business administration I have, or that I was top of my class.

I have a clear and defined handprint on my cheek, my lip is slightly busted, and my eye is bright red. I guess he caught my eye when he hit me. It doesn't hurt, but it looks like it should. "Shit," I mutter. I'm not going to be able to hide this if it bruises. I sigh and get into the shower to burn away the feeling of their hands on me.

I don't know why I do this to myself. Every night I stand in this shower and hate myself for letting men do this to me. It doesn't matter if they are rough or not. I never wanted this for myself. I never wanted to be used by everyone for money. I had completely different expectations for my life, and being a whore wasn't one of them.

I scrub my body and find that I am, in fact, bleeding from my rectum. It's not bad, but it just goes to show that I'm an idiot and shouldn't be letting men do that to me. Although that was not how things should be. Rob has rules, and they knowingly broke every single one of them. Does that make it rape? I tried to stop George, but he didn't. The other two went so hard, as if their goal was to hurt me. My screams fueled their violent thrusts.

When I give up scrubbing, I shut the water off and get out. I hear a floorboard creak, and fear rushes through me. Did I lock the door? Surely to God I did. I always do. I hurriedly pull on a giant T-shirt and step into panties before wrapping my hair. There haven't been any other noises, so maybe I was hearing things. I slowly step out of the bedroom and stop to listen.

"Hello?" I call out. "I'm sad. Perfect time to come out and kill me..."

Nothing.

I sigh and go to the kitchen right as the kettle starts screaming. I have it timed perfectly so I can get through my shower before it is done. I pour the hot water over the tea bag and let it steep while I go around the apartment and make sure everything is locked. When I get back, I add honey and take the cup to my room.

This is my nightly routine and has been since I was a teen. I drink my tea and read a book until I inevitably pass out. This sleepy-time tea kicks my ass, but I sleep so well. By the time I finish my tea, my eyes are heavy, and I am exhausted. I lay my book down on my nightstand so I don't drop it again and relax into unconsciousness.

Chapter Two
The Guardian

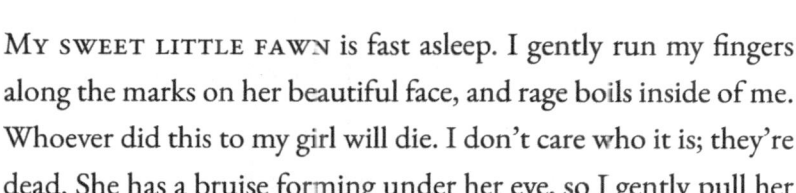

MY SWEET LITTLE FAWN is fast asleep. I gently run my fingers along the marks on her beautiful face, and rage boils inside of me. Whoever did this to my girl will die. I don't care who it is; they're dead. She has a bruise forming under her eye, so I gently pull her eyelid up to find that it is clearly irritated and blood red.

I know she dances at that club. I don't like it, but I can't go in there without being made immediately. The Treasure Chest is known for high-class hookers, and I fear that's what she's been up to. I gently pull the blanket off her, still testing to make sure the drugs I put in her kettle have taken effect. Her routine is so predictable that I can slip in through the fire escape while she is in the shower and slip it in. By the time she is in bed, she is well on her way to being mine for the evening.

Who am I kidding? She's always been mine. She will always be mine. I spend a few hours every night worshiping her body. I want so badly to fill her tight little pussy with my cock, but I won't. Not until she is awake and wants me inside of her. That doesn't stop me from feeling her, tasting her, and making her body shake as I pull orgasms out of her sleepy body. Fuck, she is so amazing, perfect in every way.

I pull her panties off and set them aside so I do not lose them. She is freshly showered, and I can smell the citrus soap on her body. Touching her is like a drug to me. I am so addicted to her and no matter how many times I tell myself that it's bad to come in here… to follow her… I can't stop. I will do anything to keep her. No one will claim my little fawn. She may not know it yet, but she belongs to me and will for as long as we both breathe and exist. Even in death, she will never escape me.

I spread her thighs, but a growl rumbles in my chest when I see that my little fawn is swollen. Upon inspection, I realize that someone has hurt her more than I thought. She's been raped recently. Her pussy is red and puffy, like she was fucked dry. She had a panty liner in her panties, but she's not even close to starting her period. I keep inspecting her body, and I turn damn near murderous when I find that she is bleeding from her ass.

"Who hurt you, Little Fawn? Who am I going to kill tonight?" I ask her, but I'm mostly talking to myself. It's not like she can hear me.

I decide that I won't be too hard on her tonight. I hate when she's in pain. Instead of fucking her with my fingers like I usually would, I gently flick my tongue across her clit. I smile when she lets out a small whimper. I love the way she responds to me. I start with soft and gentle licks before letting my tongue explore her sweet and eager little cunt. Even sore, she still seeks me out by shifting her hips in her sleep. I know how much to put in her tea so that she never wakes, so her moving like this is normal. I've learned everything about her, and I know how her body works. I know how to make her come fast and how to draw it out until her body is fucking begging for it. When I start lightly suckling on her clit, a deep, guttural moan sounds through the room, and I suck harder. Her thighs tremble, and I know she's close. She will get to a point where she is responding, but still fast asleep. Her hand lazily touches my head, and I suck hard, letting my teeth graze and nip at her clit. When she explodes, her moan is loud. I reach up and grab her throat and squeeze as I keep pulling her orgasm out. Her body goes rigid, and one orgasm blends into two before I let up.

Lori relaxes into the bed with a sigh and a small smile on her lips. I am content leaving her early tonight now. I need to handle whoever hurt her. Rob is the only one who sort of knows, but he knows I will skin him alive if he tells her that I know she works there. I get my phone out and call Rob as I pull her shirt up to expose her perfect tits. Her legs are wide open for me, so I kneel on the bed so that when I pull my cock out, I am inches from her pussy. I groan as I slowly drag the head of my cock across her entrance and rub her clit with myself. Her body jerks and I know I need to get away from her cunt before I fuck her.

"Hey, man. I was waiting for you to call," Rob answers.

"Who hurt her?" I demand.

"She... Lorelei works in the back rooms," he says carefully.

"What?" I snap.

"Hey. I'm not in the business of telling women what to do with their bodies. Sometimes they get rough, but never like this. I've never had anyone do this before. She has never been hurt like this before," he explains. "His name is George Fallon. He apparently snuck two buddies in tonight with him. He's been seeing her every weekend since she started. He's usually pretty tame, but... I pulled the tapes for that room.

"Send it to me," I growl.

"I don't know if you want to see this," Rob remarks.

"Whatever the price... I'll pay. I want to know who it is I'm killing," I say.

"Okay. Okay," he sighs. "You should have it, but keep me out of it, please."

"I will," I say.

"Me and one of the bouncers finally have her talked out of working back there. Omar watches over her, and he has been trying for months to get her to quit. I think we are pretty close," he says. "She's done in the back, though. I think tonight scared her enough that she is done."

"Good," I say. "I'll keep your name out of it. Just send me what you have on these fuckers, please."

"To the burner?"

"Yes, Rob."

"Got it. His whole folder is sent over," he says.

"Thanks." I end the call and fist my cock to start fucking my hand. It's not enough. I open the video and watch as I keep stroking myself. When he starts to violently fuck her throat, I want to feel her mouth on me. I prop my phone up so I can move it up to my face. I listen to the sounds of her muffled screams as I gently open her mouth.

"They'll fucking die for this, Little Fawn. I own you, and no one touches what's mine," I growl as I slowly push into her mouth. My balls tighten when she wraps her lips around my cock and sleepily sucks, as if it's an instinct. Her eyes are closed, so she's doing this in her sleep. "Oh, baby girl. Fucking perfect."

I reposition her body so I can hold her head between my hands as it dangles off the edge of the bed. I push down her throat, and she keeps sucking as I rock my hips in small strokes. I want to live in this woman's body. I've never felt something so fucking amazing. I promised myself that the first time I fucked someone, it would be her, and she would be well aware of what I was doing to her. The downside to being a virgin is that I fear I will disappoint her. I want the first time that we fuck to be the best sex of her life. I know that she has had other partners, but I want to be the best of all of them. I made a promise to myself that her cunt and ass were off-limits while she sleeps, but the rest of her is free game. My sweet little fawn sucks cock in her sleep. Can she be any more perfect?

"Fuck," I hiss as my body jerks. I pull out of her mouth and fuck my fist, her saliva acting as a lubricant. When I finally come, it all lands on her tits and chest like an artwork of my devotion to her. This woman owns me just as much as I own her. I've saved myself for her, and as much as I would like to kill each and every person who even looks at her, I won't control what she does with her body. I will still rip apart anyone who causes her pain without her consent, though.

I reposition her in bed and clean her body. I lay in the bed with her for a moment once I have her dressed. She's still sleeping peacefully, but when her body senses mine, she automatically turns and snuggles against my chest. Fuck, I love this woman so goddamn much. I'm getting to the point where I know that I need to speak up and let her know that I'm here. I've always been here, and I always will be. I have two very distinct parts of my personality. This side, the side that hunts her from the shadows and enjoys her body at night, doesn't want to give her any other choice but to learn to love me the way I love her. The man I am during the day wants her to have the free will to go where life takes her.

Does she know how many times she has come for me? Does she know how I have kept her safe for years until now? I failed her by letting her be in that fucking club. I should've ended that before it ever got this bad. I know Lorelei, and I can't imagine she truly wants to be letting random men use her body. Who am I to judge, though? I just throat-fucked the girl in her sleep. Does that make me as bad as the man who hurt her tonight? The difference is, I love her. She knows one part of me, but it's time she starts to get to know this side.

I'M STANDING OUTSIDE THE home of George Fallon. The two men from the video that fucked my girl are resting in the living room with him. Originally, I was going to come in and just shoot all three of them, but that would leave evidence. Instead, I'm going in with a wooden bat. When I get done obliterating their fucking heads, I'll burn it in my fireplace at home.

I pull on my neon purge mask and open the back door. You see, men like this think they are invincible. They would never imagine that someone would come in and hurt them. Women are sure to lock their doors, and they always double-check, but not George. Lorelei always double-checks her doors and windows at night, but she doesn't know that I can get into the fire escape regardless of a lock.

I slowly creep through the house until I get to the living room. Two of them are on the couch and one is in the armchair, but they are all facing away from me. They have beers in their hands, and an empty liquor bottle is on the coffee table. Good, they are drunk. It will be less of a fight if they are shitfaced.

The two on the couch are the ones who raped her, but I start with the man on the right. I need to make my hits count so that they don't come after me all at once. I line up my bat, and with one fatal swing, it cracks into the side of his head before anyone can react. I immediately rear back and swing down hard, hitting the man on the left directly in the temple. They both collapse, and the man in the armchair, George Fallon, is on his feet.

"You're a dead bitch," he growls. He goes for the pistol in his waistband that I already spotted, but as soon as he pulls it, I swing the bat and knock it out of his hand. He screams in pain when bones in his wrist audibly crack. "Fuck. What the fuck did you do?!"

"You hurt my girl," I growl. "She doesn't belong to you."

"What? Is this about that whore from the club?"

"She's not a whore," I scream at him as I swing the bat again and make contact with his ribs. He screams out as he falls to the ground, immediately shielding his face when I stand over him with my bat raised in the air. "She's *mine*."

"Wait, stop!" he pleads, but it's too late. The moment he touched Lorelei Belmont, he was a fucking dead man. No one touches my girl. No one.

I slam the bat down on the top of his head, and I keep swinging over and over again until there's nothing left. His face and head are obliterated, brain matter spilling out of his skull. I hear one of the men behind me groan, so I spin around and swing the bat again. He was standing and attempting to flee, but I sent him crashing into the glass coffee table. I give him the same treatment and start slamming the bat down on his head until the sight of his blood and brains satisfies me. The other one might be dead, but I don't leave survivors. He is slumped on the couch, but as I get closer, I see that he is still breathing. It is shallow and labored, so I line the bat up with the center of his face. I recognize him as the one who hit her. He was mad that she was sobbing. Pathetic. I smash the bat against his face, and I keep hitting him until I release all of my anger.

I'm fucking amazed that the bat has held up through three skulls, but it will be easier to transport without it being splintered. I'm covered in blood, but I have made sure not to step in any of it. I also have gloves on, so I search for a trash bag to put the bat in before walking out of the house. I'm confident that I did not leave any evidence behind, so I will just have to burn everything I'm wearing, along with the bat.

I get back to my truck and I already have trash bags and protective liners laid out so I can sit in the truck without getting blood on anything. I turn on the music and let it drown out any negative feelings I have toward this. It had to be done because it hurt her. I will play the devil so long as she continues to be my sweet angel. She is the definition of perfection, and I won't allow anyone to taint that.

Once I get to the house, I start a fire in the fireplace and toss everything in. I sit and watch as the last of the evidence burns, content with what I have done.

Chapter Three
Lorelei

"Well, looks like you aren't the only one he pissed off," Tris laughs. Beatris Cooper is my best friend and the only one who knows that I work at the club. She was not aware that I was fucking men for money, but she knows now. Luckily, she doesn't judge.

"Would Omar really do this?" I ask as I read through the article.

"Shit, I don't know. If he was that protective of you. Maybe?" she says. "But they could have just pissed someone else off."

"They are just calling it a home invasion, so maybe it was random," I say.

"Don't stress. You didn't kill them," she says. "Also, why the fuck didn't you call me, Lori?"

"I just... I don't know. I just wanted to go to sleep," I say. "I am still incredibly sore today. I knew I would be. It's not as bad as yesterday, luckily. I stayed in bed all weekend."

"How bad is it?" she asks.

"I'm literally swollen down there," I say quieter when I hear Cameron, my brother, outside the office door.

"Ouch," she says.

"Hey, Cam," I say when he walks into my office.

"Hey. Sorry, I know you're on lunch," he says. "Can you join us for a meeting at one? Usually, we can take notes pretty well, but…"

"Cam, I already told you and Remy that you need to start having me join all the meetings. You should be focusing on that, and I will handle everything else. Okay? You do best with the nerdy shit, and I do better with the administrative shit."

"I just make pretty pictures," Tris grins. She works in marketing and leads all the graphics and marketing teams. Her degree is in graphic design and marketing, so it's the perfect fit for her.

"I just don't want you to feel like you have to do everything," Cam says.

"Cam," I sigh. "My name is on the fucking building, too. You tell me I have every right to claim this business too, so let me do my job. This is what I went to school to do. The moment you started your company, I wanted to be right here helping you two. So, I am coming to meetings and doing my job."

"Okay. Okay," he says. "You okay? You have been holed up in here all day."

"Yeah." I smile. "We are done eating, so we can walk back with you to prep for the meeting. I haven't had a chance to bug Remy today."

"Yeah. He was worried about you when you didn't come to family dinner last night," Cam says. I stand and gather my stuff before we walk out of my office. Theirs is just next door, so we don't have far to go.

"Yeah, I just wasn't feeling well," I say. "We still doing dinner tonight?"

"Yeah. Mom and Dad are making ribs," Cam says.

"Ah. Perfect," I say as we walk into his and Remy's office.

Remington and Cameron own Saltz & Belmont Technologies. They started it in college, and it has grown from little computer repair businesses into a full-blown software company. I think they're the nerdiest and humblest millionaires ever. They are both set to be billionaires in the next five years, but they act like they live paycheck to paycheck. To be fair, I do too. I make six figures working for them and another five grand a week at the club.

"Hey, Remy," I say sweetly.

"Hey, Lori," he says, matching my smile. Remy is the sweetest and gentlest man I have ever met. He is kind and compassionate, but he has a nasty temper. I've only ever seen it once when I was raped by a classmate in high school. I called him when I snuck out to a party after I was cornered and raped bloody by the quarterback of the football team. He told Cameron, and when they showed up, I really thought they were going to murder him. After that, his parents abruptly moved across the state in the middle of senior year, and I never went to another party.

Remy is big and muscly but wears these reading glasses that are admittedly hot as fuck. God, when he looks up at me over the top rim of them with a straight face? Fucking *swoon*. He doesn't even see it, though. He is so damn innocent. I can be a brat to him all day long, and he will just call me silly. Occasionally I hit a nerve, and he will just bearhug me and tickle my sides until I nearly piss myself. I think that Remy is the absolute love of my life, but a man like him deserves so much more than a whore who has been run through by all of New York City.

"How are you?" I ask.

"I am well," he says as he stands and hugs me tightly. Fuck, I love his hugs. I could live here in his arms. "How are you?"

"I'm okay," I say quietly.

"What's wrong?" he asks with a concerned tone as he lifts my chin.

"Ah, just cramps," I lie.

"I'm sorry," he frowns. "Anything I can do?"

"No. Just one of those things," I smile. "You coming to dinner tonight?"

"I sure am," he says.

"You coming tonight?" Cam asks Tris.

"I mean, I already have once today. I could go for another," she says, and I laugh heartily.

"What?" Cam asks. Tris and I laugh more at their innocence. Tris has been hitting on Cameron for years, and he is so fucking oblivious. I keep telling her she needs to be straight up and just tell him she likes him, but I think she's just as nervous.

"Oh, Cam," I say, giggling. I am surprised to see Remy smirking, so I narrow my eyes at him. "What are you smiling at?"

"You, silly girl. Are you two being dirty?"

"I didn't say anything. I'm innocent," I say, making Tris snort. "Cam is just oblivious."

"To what?" Cam asks, confused.

"Yes, she will be at dinner tonight, Cameron," I laugh. "So, this meeting?"

"Uhm. Right," Cam says, refocusing.

I PULL INTO MOM and Dad's driveway and park beside Remy. Tris parks beside me, and we go inside. "Hey, Momma," I say as I kiss her cheek.

"Hey, baby girl," she says as she sets the wooden spoon down and hugs me. "You feeling better?"

"Mmm. I'm okay," I say.

"You're a terrible liar," she says softly. As someone walks into the kitchen.

"Hey," Dad says happily.

"Hey, Daddy!" I say as I turn and hug him.

"How are you?"

"I'm okay," I say.

"Remy is looking for you, by the way," Mom says as she hugs Tris.

"Staying out of trouble, Tris?" Dad asks as he hugs her next.

"Ha. No," she laughs.

"She was flirting with Cam again today, and it went right over his head," I laugh.

"That boy," Mom laughs.

"It would be easier to just tell him," I tell Tris.

"This is fun though," she laughs.

"Until he figures it out and fucks you up for teasing him for so long," I laugh.

"Cam? Nah," she says. "He's a big teddy bear."

"I said the same thing about Bill, and then I limped for a week," Mom says casually. Dad gasps in shock at her, but we all laugh heartily. Cam and Remy walk in from the back patio and look confused.

"What's up?" Cam asks.

"Just talking about Dad railing Mom," Tris laughs.

"Sorry I asked," he laughs. "Hey, Sis."

"Hey, Cam," I smile. "You were looking for me, Remy?"

"Yeah. Come outside with me," he says, motioning for me to follow him. I walk back through the house and out onto the front porch before he speaks again.

"Everything okay?" I ask.

"Yeah. I just got something for you," he says. "Also, I explained to Cam what Tris has been doing."

"Oh no," I laugh as we stop at Remy's truck. "I told her to talk to him instead of teasing him."

"Well, she's about to learn a lesson about why she shouldn't be a brat to Cameron," he laughs and picks me up to sit me in the driver's seat. He reaches past me, pressing his body against mine, to grab a bag. He is so nonchalant about it; there's no way he gets how... intimate that is.

"Mmm. Yeah. Someone should take that girl down a few notches," I say.

"Someone should take *you* down a few notches," he teases.

"Are you volunteering, Remy?" I ask with a sweet smile. His face reddens and I giggle as I pat his cheek.

"You are a silly girl, Lori," he says, grabbing my hand and kissing my palm.

Remy opens the bag to look inside before handing it to me. "What's this?" I ask.

"Well, you said cramps were bothering you. I know they can get pretty bad for you, so I just got you a few things to hopefully help," he says. "Didn't want to make a big deal of it in there, so I thought out here was better."

I look in the bag and he has bought everything from Midol, to chocolate, to a heating pad, and even pads. "Remington, you didn't have to do this," I say. "Thank you."

"I know, but I wanted to," he says as he hugs me. I bury my face in his neck and hold on to him. Tears suddenly surface, and he notices before I can stop it. "Hey. What's wrong?"

Remy pulls back and holds my face as I choke back tears. "Nothing," I lie.

"Lori," he says softly. "What's wrong?"

"You're so fucking innocent, Remy. You'll judge, and I can't be judged by you. Cam is one thing, but not you," I sniff as tears roll down my cheeks.

"Come on, Lori," he encourages. "I won't judge you."

"In college... I worked at The Treasure Club for fun. I danced for money. I still work there on Friday and Saturdays... but... I... fuck."

"Deep breathe and try again," he says softly.

"I let men fuck me for money," I say bluntly as I fight back the urge to sob.

"Did something happen?" he asks, and I nod.

"A client that has come in every week since I started brought two friends. He's never been violent with me, but last night, he was. I tried to stop him, but he wouldn't," I cry. "They hurt me."

"Oh, honey," he says as he hugs me against his chest. He lets me cry and doesn't say anything until I calm down again. "I don't know why I do this to myself. I hate being there. I hate letting people do that."

"It's hypersexuality, Lorelei. It's a response to trauma," he says. "Just because you respond that way doesn't mean you always like it. Doesn't mean they had the right to hurt you."

"I'm scared of not being there. I enjoy dancing. It's an escape," I say. "But the rest..."

"Well, rent out a space so you can be alone and dance. You make enough to do it, so use that hoard of cash you have," he says. "Dance however you want to whatever music you like and just escape."

"Yeah," I sniff. "I think there is a studio a few blocks from me."

"Why would I judge you for getting hurt?" he asks, wiping my tears away.

"Because you are so sweet and innocent," I say. "Men like you..."

"Before you slut-shame yourself, understand my patience only goes so far, Lorelei," he warns.

"What are you going to do? Frown harder at me?" I ask, and he chuckles.

"Lori, it is not my place to judge you for what you do with your body. I will judge the fact that they hurt you, though."

"I kinda skipped a part," I say.

"What?" he asks.

"I saw an article this morning that those three men were found dead after a home invasion. Apparently, they were connected to the mafia or something," I say. "I feel responsible."

"Well, did you kill them?" he asks.

"No," I laugh.

"Then it sounds like karma, Lori. You are not responsible for what others do," he says. "If they hurt you, who's to say they haven't hurt someone else? I'm sure their list of enemies is not isolated to just you."

"Yeah. That's what Tris said," I say.

"So, is it not cramps?" he asks carefully.

"No," I sigh. "Just a long irritation. They used condoms, thankfully. Fucking dry is not comfortable."

"What do you need?" he asks.

"Remington, you are not responsible for my wounded genitalia," I say, and he laughs heartily.

"I know that, but I want to help. I assume Cam doesn't know?"

"No," I say. "Just my boss, a friend at the club, and Tris found out today. Well, now you know."

"I'll talk to Cam," he offers.

"He knew I danced, but... The clients that come in there to get laid... They are like... billionaire executives," I say. "George paid me ten thousand last night."

"Shit," he says.

"Is that bad?" I ask. "That's bad, isn't it?"

"Uh... I won't lie, Lori. If anyone connects you... Let me talk to Cam and we can go from there. Once I know he won't go and burn the building down, we can all sit down and make a plan."

"I'm going to have to tell Mom and Dad, aren't I?" I ask.

"Mmmm... Yeah," he says. "Just in case it gets out, but let's handle Cam first."

"Okay," I sigh. "I didn't even think it could hurt the company... I'm sorry, Remy."

"It's okay," he smiles. "We will figure it out, no matter what happens."

"We should get back," I say. Remy lifts me and sets me on my feet so I can put the bag in my car. When I turn back around, Remy hugs me before kicking his door shut.

"Let's go see how fucked up Tris is now," he chuckles.

Chapter Four

Beatris

"Walk with me," Cam says when his parents are distracted. He takes my hand and leads me onto the back patio and out into the yard.

"What's up?" I ask.

"Just wanted to talk. Thought we could walk the trail," he says, keeping hold of my hand.

"Whatcha wanna talk about?" I ask.

"So, Remy tells me that you have been flirting with me for quite a while, and I have been oblivious," he says. Heat floods my face, and I say nothing as we walk deeper into the woods. "Surely you have something to say, Tris."

"There are easier ways to reject me than to kill me in the woods, Cam," I say. He abruptly turns and pushes me back against a huge tree before placing his hands on either side of my waist. He is nearly pressed against me, and I realize I have severely underestimated this man.

"Instead of teasing me when you know I don't understand, why didn't you just come to me?" he asks. "You know social cues aren't exactly my forte, Tris. Why be a brat?"

"I was scared," I admit quietly.

"Of what?" His voice softens, but he doesn't move an inch.

"You, I guess," I say. "I was afraid you'd reject me because I'm your little sister's friend."

My breath catches in my throat when he leans into my body and his lips brush mine. "Say it," he says softly.

"I like you," I whisper. "A lot."

"Oh, you can do better than that," he says with a wicked smile before kissing me hard. When he pulls back, I am dazed. I might regret saying this, but screw it.

"Fuck me," I say. "Please."

Cam turns me before pushing me past the wood line a bit. When he stops, I am immediately bent over a large fallen tree. "Cam!" I yelp when he pushes my skirt up and rips my panties off.

"You know how long I have wanted to do this, Tris?" he rumbles as he unbuttons his jeans. "You know how many times I have fantasized about bending your bratty ass over and fucking you?"

"As much as I have," I choke out. When he grabs my hips, I panic slightly. "Wait, I'm not on birth control, Cam."

"Good," he growls before slamming into me. I gasp and lap my hand over my mouth as I put my other hand on the ground to stabilize myself as he starts to rail into me. "Fuck, you're so goddamn tight."

"Oh, dear God. Cam. Fuck... You're too big," I whimper. "I can't..."

"Oh, you can take it. My sweet little fuck toy, you wanted this," he growls. He is stretching me, and my body struggles to adapt as he quickens his pace and fucks me harder.

"Oh fuck. Oh fuck," I moan. "Fuck, I love your cock. Oh my God, Cam."

"You're mine, Tris. Got it?" he says, emphasizing his words with punishing thrusts.

"Yes. Oh, God. Yes," I say. He grabs me by the hair to pull my head up so he can cover my mouth. He starts pounding into me so hard that all I can do is scream against his hand as he fucks a blinding orgasm out of me. Cam groans as he fills me with come, and we are both left panting and breathless.

Cam helps me stand and brushes the dirt off my clothing and legs before kissing me again. "Sorry," he smirks.

"For what? Nearly fucking me to death? Where did that come from, Cam?" I ask. "I mean... Do it again, but shit."

"You are mine," Cam says firmly. "None of this bullshit where you are too afraid to talk to me. You want me. I want you, so now we have each other. Okay?"

"Okay," I smile. "Are we...telling the others?"

"Remy... I doubt he will connect it, but Lori definitely will. Let's just get settled as an 'us' first, and then we can tell them," he says, kissing me again.

"Can I get late-night booty calls?" I ask with a grin.

"Beatris, when I say you are mine, I mean you are going to have your happy ass in my bed every night," he says. "If you want a late-night fuck, just roll over and take what you want."

"Oh, please tell me you'll do the same," I laugh.

"You want me to fuck you awake, pretty girl?" he asks with a conniving grin.

"God, yes," I reply happily.

"Safe word?" he asks.

"Uh... Apricot. Why?"

"Because I'm going to fuck you until you don't want it, and then I'm going to keep going until you call it," he says before kissing me. "When you are a brat to me, I'm going to fuck you each and every time. How nice do you think I'll be when I put you on your knees?"

"You, sir, are…" I start to say.

"Shocking? Yeah. I know," he smiles. "I keep my shit tucked away."

"We should head back," I say. "Your come is starting to drip down my thighs."

"Let's go," he laughs.

"Is Remy into Lori?" I ask. "Between us."

"Between us? He is in love with her," he says. "But… He is a virgin, so it's like a roadblock for him."

"I figured you were the virgin," I say, and he laughs. "Does he think she will judge him?"

"I mean, He's twenty-nine, so I think at this point, yeah. It's not that he doesn't know what he's doing, because he does. He's just never wanted to have sex."

"So, he's like… Saving himself?"

"Yeah, I think so. He's messed around with girls before, and he's done everything except sex. He just never lets it progress," Cam explains. "Eventually, he will slip up and Lori will catch it. Once he knows that she won't judge him, he will chill."

"And probably fuck her to death," I laugh.

"His name was horse dick in high school for a reason," he laughs. "Is Lori okay, by the way?"

"Uh..."

"I'll take that as a no."

"I'm... She's my best friend," I say.

"I'm not asking you to betray her, Tris. Is she safe? I haven't seen her this withdrawn in a while."

"She's safe," I confirm. "You'll need to talk to her if you want to know more, though."

"I understand," he says as he stops and looks at me. "Never feel like you have to choose a side. She is your best friend, and I will never get in the way of that. I only ask you to come to me if she is in danger or might be eventually. I don't care if you tell her about us, but just don't use her as a middleman if we are arguing, and I won't either."

"She'd tell us both to fuck off," I laugh as I go up on my tiptoes and kiss him. "Can I come over tonight?"

"You sure can," he smiles.

Chapter Five
Lorelei

"Leaving so soon?" Mom asks when I grab my bag.

"Momma, it's late," I laugh. "I need to get some sleep."

"Are you okay?" she asks.

"I am," I say. "I'll explain, I just need time to process."

"Okay, baby. Well, call me tomorrow," she says.

"I will. Bye, Dad," I say as he comes into the living room.

"Bye, sweetheart," he says as he hugs me.

"Boo," Tris says.

"Leaving?" Remy asks.

"Mhmm," I smile.

"I'll walk you out," he says.

"See you in the morning, sis," Cam says.

"Bye."

We walk outside, and Remy opens my driver's side door for me. I lean down and toss my bag in before turning back to look at him. "What's up?" I ask.

"What can I do?" he asks. "It feels wrong to just let you go home and be alone with all of that."

"You are so sweet, Remy," I say with a smile. "Really though, I'm okay. I'll just boil myself in the shower again, drink some tea, read, and then go to sleep like I do every night."

"Text me, okay?" he asks. "I worry about you."

"I'll text you, no need to worry about me, Remy. You worry about getting a girlfriend so you can spoil her as much as you spoil me," I say. He chuckles and wraps me in a hug. "I appreciate you so much, Remy. You are the calm I need."

"I'm always here," he says, kissing the top of my head. "Have a good night, Lori. Remember, you are not a lobster. Don't boil yourself."

"Damn. Wish I was. That would be a hell of a suicide," I laugh as I turn to get in the car. I gasp when he suddenly yanks me back and slams me against my car. "It was a joke! Dark joke. I'm kidding. I'm sorry."

"Damn," I hear Tris laugh.

"Don't ever let me hear you say something like that again, Lorelei," Remy says with a grave tone.

"Or what?" I challenge him with a sweet smile. "Are you going to punish me, Remy?"

"Someone ought to," he frowns.

"You'd think after last night I'd learn better than to tempt a man," I say, laughing at my own fucked-up joke. The growl that comes out of this man makes my knees weak as he gets in my face.

"I have been so fucking patient with you, Lori. Keep pushing me," he warns with a gritty tone. I surprise him when I lean forward and whisper in his ear.

"Be careful, Remington. I have more experience than you," I say softly before kissing his cheek.

"Goodnight, Lorelei," he grunts before stepping back.

"Good to know that threatening you with a whore is the trick to outsmarting you," I say. I squeal and jump into my car before he can grab me, making Cam and Tris laugh as they watch. I wave and smile sweetly at Remy when he tries to open my door, but finds that it's locked. He glares as he watches me back out and eventually throws his hand up to wave goodbye as I pull off.

I know what I need to do, but it requires me to go up to the club. I am not having this conversation over the phone, so it's easier if I just go up there. When I pull into the lot, it's relatively slow. When I walk inside, Dazzle, one of the dancers, smiles at me.

"Hey, girl!" she says as she hugs me.

"Hey," I say. "Rob around?"

"Yeah. He's on the floor somewhere."

"Thanks," I say before walking past her and onto the main floor. The familiar music thumps through the room and the usual stench of alcohol and cigarette smoke permeates the room.

"You better be fucking joking," I hear Omar say. I turn around and smile at him, and he hugs me. "What the fuck are you doing here, Lorelei?"

"I need to talk to Rob. Wanna sit in?" I ask.

"Yeah. Come on," he replies loud enough that we can hear over the music. He throws his hand up and motions to Rob, who has just stepped out of the back dressing room.

When we get into Rob's office, the door shuts, and we can finally hear. "What are you doing here?" Rob asks me.

"Who killed them?" I ask. He just stares at me because he knows what I am talking about.

"What?" Omar asks.

"George and his two friends that raped me. Who killed them?" I ask again.

"Oh fuck. I wish it was me. How'd they die?" he asks.

"Article just said a home invasion, and they have ties to the mafia," I say. "Rob?"

"I did not," he says.

"But you know who did?" I ask.

"Uh…"

"Rob," I snap. "Am I responsible for this?"

"No," he says firmly. "This is not on you. They died because they are low-life pieces of shit, Lorelei."

"Why won't you tell me?"

"Because I will be next," he says. "They are dead. No one is going to jail for it. End of story."

"I quit," I say.

"Thank God," Omar says, hugging me tightly. When he pulls back, Rob smiles.

"I can't keep doing this to myself. I opened up to someone today, and I'm realizing that I am doing this to myself as a result of something that happened when I was a teen. I am going to rent a space so I can still dance when I want, just alone where no one can grope me," I explain. "I'm going to focus on my job and my family and stop torturing myself."

"Good," Rob smiles.

"I don't know how I feel about you two being so happy," I say.

"Baby, you are so much better than this place. You have a fucking master's," Omar says. "There is nothing wrong with what happens here, but you have bigger shit to be doing than taking your clothes off for drunk men."

"Was I at least missed Saturday?" I ask.

"You were," Rob says. "Another regular. I think his name was Thomas. He came in for you, but I let him know that you were no longer working here. He was sad but then went and fucked Jazzy."

"Oh, well okay," I laugh. "He tips well."

"Ha," Omar laughs.

"I'm going to go home now," I say.

"Well, be safe. Call if you need anything, okay?" Omar says. "We will have to meet up for lunch one day."

"Okay," I smile. "Bye, guys."

"Bye, Lorelei," Rob says, hugging me. Omar hugs me next before I leave. I hurry to my car before I start crying.

I don't know why I am upset. I only liked being here for the dancing, and I have a plan. I'll go up there tomorrow and handle it, so it won't be that big of a deal. It doesn't stop me from crying all the way home. When I park, I am sniffling as I go inside and step into the elevator. At the last second, a man steps in. When I look up, I can only see his back. He says nothing and has his hood up, so I assume it's my late-night friend who never speaks. I am usually too exhausted to pay attention to how tall he is. He is kind of hunched over, though, so I can't really tell exactly how tall he is. When we get to my floor and the doors open, I step past without a word. A familiar scent hits me, and I spin around to see the doors shut.

Weird.

When I step into my apartment, I pull my phone out and text Remy as I get ready to take a bath. My body is sore, so I think relaxing will do me some good. Once the kettle is on, I go into the bathroom to fill up the old clawfoot tub.

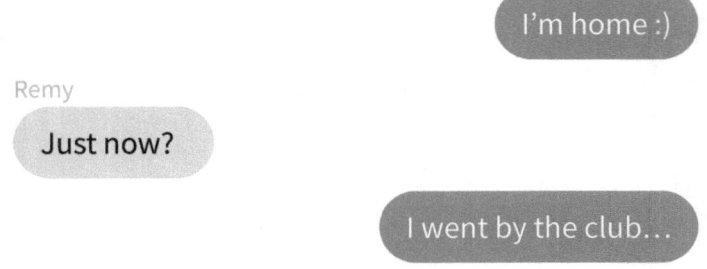

Remy

> Oh? What for?

I quit and then sobbed the whole way home. I think I'm broken.

> Not broken, just traumatized. Closing chapters of your life can be taxing. What are you doing?

Wishing I was a lobster.

> Brat :(

I'm getting ready for bed lol. Going to drink tea and read. Think tea and a muscle relaxer is a bad combo?

> If you have to question it, maybe don't lol.

That's fair. Tea acquired. In the bath now. What are you doing?

> Just texting you. Can I ask you something?

Go for it.

Remy

> You always call me innocent. Is that a bad thing? I can't tell if it's a stab at me or if you are just playing.

>> It's not bad at all, Remy. You are the sweetest man I have literally ever known. Innocent does not mean bad. It just means you have not been ruined by the world like I have been.

> It also means inexperienced, Lori. Also, you are not ruined.

>> Inexperienced just means you need a good teacher ;) I feel ruined. My lady bits are swollen, dude. Too much info, I know.

> You are not ruined, and you will heal, Lori. Do you need anything?

>> Just getting really sleepy right now. I need to get out of the bath and get into bed. This tea kicks my ass. Probably should have waited until after bath time.

> Get out before you drown yourself.

I am so fucking sleepy that I can't get myself up out of the bath. My sleepy mind is panicked because the bath is full, and I am slowly slipping down. I fight with my body to pull the plug out of the drain. Just as I slip under the water, I feel the plug come out of the drain.

Chapter Six
Remington

THIS GIRL IS GOING to give me heart problems. I step into her bathroom as the tub is emptying. I pull her head up out of the water and let the tub empty before scooping her into my arms. On the way out of the bathroom, I grab her towels and take her into her room.

In hindsight, I should have paid attention to whether she was showering or taking a bath before I treated her tea, but I'm always here when I do it. She never takes a bath, though. Right now, is the point I should feel bad because I could have hurt her, but she was never in danger. I do know that I can't play with her like I usually would because she will then know that it's me. I will just tell her that I got concerned that she didn't text back and came over. The girl doesn't even know she's being followed by anyone, so she won't think anything of it.

I work on drying her off before dressing her. I think it's adorable that she wears my shirts to bed, but also, how does she have my shirts? I haven't seen some of these in months.

"Remy?" she mutters.

"Yeah, it's me," I say as I pull the shirt over her head.

"I'm naked," she sighs. I'm not fully convinced that she is awake. I didn't give her as much as I usually do because I didn't know if she took a muscle relaxer like she had mentioned. The last thing I want to do is make her overdose.

"Not for long. I've got you," I say.

"I was scared."

"You're safe," I say. I move her up on the bed so I can cover her up and she grabs my wrist.

"Will you stay with me?" she asks. I sit down and I see that she is awake, and her eyes are open. I kick my shoes off and lie beside her, and she smiles weakly at me. "Thank you."

"Anytime." I smile back at her as I tuck my arm under my head to prop up slightly. I am making sure not to touch her. When she shifts closer, I move back.

"I don't have hooker cooties," she says with a deep frown.

"I didn't say you did," I say as I grab her hips and pull her against me. I instantly regret it when she throws her leg over top of mine and blood rushes to my cock. Fuck, I need to chill. This girl doesn't have panties on. "You can't do that to me, Lori."

"Why? Afraid I'll ruin you?" she asks.

"No, you don't have panties on and there are parts of me that act without permission." I say honestly.

"Ohhhh," she says sleepily. She looks high as fuck, so I am pretty sure she did take a muscle relaxer. The sedative just isn't strong enough to keep her asleep. "So, you are afraid of my pussy?"

"I am not," I say with a smirk.

"It won't bite you, Remy,"

"I am aware," I say with a laugh.

"If you aren't scared... Then I must be turning you on," she says, intentionally pressing herself against my cock. I groan and she giggles.

"Lori," I say. I don't want her to think I am rejecting her, but I refuse to fuck her when she is like this. It's one thing when she is out of it. She has no idea what I've done... Fuck, I am not better than the men who violently hurt her... I keep those parts of myself separate for a reason... and this is the reason. I feel like a monster right now because the two worlds are colliding.

"What?" she asks. "Do you not want me?"

"Fuuuck," I hiss when she presses herself against me again. She lets out a little gasp and I know she felt me. "Lori, baby. You need to heal and not be high out of your mind. How many muscle relaxers did you take?"

"Mmmm. Too many," she says.

"What?" I snap. "How many, Lorelei?"

"Two, silly. Relax," she says, poking the end of my nose.

"You are going to regret this in the morning," I say.

"Why? Because I'm being a hoe, and you are sweetly rejecting me?"

"Why are you mean to yourself?" I ask.

"Why are you offended by being called innocent?" she counters.

"I'm not offended."

"Yes, you are," she retorts.

"No..."

"Yes," she huffs.

"Lori, I'm a virgin," I say, and she stops talking.

Lori is looking at me. I can't tell if she has zoned out or if she is thinking. I don't know why the fuck I said that. That is not how

I wanted to tell her. How do you tell someone that you are nearly thirty and haven't fucked anyone because you've decided you are going to save that part of yourself for them?

"You just need a teacher," she says finally. "Someone to tell you what to do."

"Is that right?" I ask.

"Mhmm. I know a girl with lots of experience," she smiles.

"Is she currently high on muscle relaxers?" I ask, and she giggles. "Lori, this is a conversation that should happen when you are not high."

"What if I don't remember?"

"Then the next time I tell you, I get to see if it's just being high that made you not laugh at me." I say.

"Why would I laugh?" she says with a frown. "If I could go back, I would have waited to have sex."

"Oh?" I ask.

"Mhmm... Before the rape... I was convinced that you'd be my first," she says. "Dumb, I know... But then he hurt me... now I'm ruined."

"You are not ruined," I say, cupping her cheek. "What if I told you that I haven't because I want you to be my first?"

"I'd make a good teacher," she says with a grin.

"Oh, would you teach me?" I ask.

"Well, I'd walk you through it. I'd tell you what I like and eventually, you'd be an expert at fucking me," she says. "Oh, and I'd definitely suck your dick. Every man should experience that."

"Noted," I laugh. "You should sleep."

"Are you going to be here when I wake?"

"No, I need to go home so I can get ready for work," I say. "I'll stay until you fall back asleep."

"Mkay," she says. She snuggles closer, but leaves her leg over mine. "I'm sleepy."

"Then sleep," I say. "I'm right here."

"I'm going to hate myself tomorrow," she says as her eyes flutter closed. The sad part is, there is nothing I can do to keep her from hating herself when she remembers how freely she spoke.

Chapter Seven
Lorelei

MY EYES SNAP OPEN when the alarm on my phone starts screaming throughout the room. It is plugged into the charger on my nightstand. I am dressed in Remy's shirt, and last night starts to come back in flashes.

"Oh no," I say as I sit up.

"What?" Tris asks, walking into the room. I scream and toss myself out of bed, not expecting her to be here. "Damn, girl."

"Fuck, Tris," I say. "When the fuck did you get here?"

"About an hour ago," she laughs. "Remy said you took a muscle relaxer and nearly drowned yourself. He went home to get a shower for work and asked me to come make sure you were good."

"I fucked up," I say as I get off of the floor.

"Uh oh," she says. I go through the evening and tell her everything that I remember.

"I... what the fuck is wrong with me?" I ask.

"Are you skipping over the fact that he is a virgin and was saving himself for you? That is cute as fuck," she says.

"I was out of my mind. Maybe I am remembering wrong," I say.

"No... Cam told me yesterday when we went for a walk that he is," she says. "Also, you brother monster fucked me in the woods."

"I'm sorry... What?" I ask.

"He fucked me... hard... over a fallen tree... and then again in his bed, on his couch, just... everywhere," she says.

"Well damn. It's about time," I laugh.

"Pretty sure he's going to get me pregnant. He knows I'm not on birth control. I told him and he said 'good' then just fucking slammed into me. Did I mention he has a giant dick and my belly hurts today?"

"That was more than I needed to know about my big brother, but good for him," I say. "And you, I guess."

"So, you aren't mad?" she asks.

"Why would I be? It just means one day you'll be my real sister," I say with a smile.

My phone dings and I glance over to see that it is Remy. I groan and pick it up to see that he texted me.

> Remy
>
> **Morning. Feeling okay?**

Yeah. Thanks for not letting me drown.

> **Not a problem. You good?**

Uh…

> **I assume you remember then.**

Yeah. I need to get ready for work.

> **Lori. We should talk today.**

I toss my phone onto my bed and start getting ready for work. Tris watches me, but doesn't say anything. She occasionally looks at her phone, but I just focus on getting ready for work.

Once I am ready, I skip coffee and breakfast and leave the apartment while Tris is in the bathroom. I can't handle today, and I am ready to go back to bed already. For the entire drive to work, I blare music to try and drown out the noise in my brain. It works until I have to go inside. Remy's truck is here already.

"Great," I mutter to myself as I walk into the building. I see him talking to someone in the lobby, but I go straight for the elevator. I get inside and the doors are about to close when he puts his hand in the way and they open.

"Good morning to you too," he says with a smile as the doors close. Instead of engaging, I pull my phone out and doom scroll on social media until the elevator opens again. I slip out and go straight for my office, shutting the door before he can get to me.

I sit at my desk and close my eyes for a moment. I need to just chill out, and everything will go back to normal in a few days. He will forget that I threw myself at him like a cheap crack whore, and all will be well.

"What?" I snap when my door comes open.

"Damn. Sorry," Cam laughs.

"Sorry," I sigh.

"I brought you coffee, since you ditched Tris," he says, sitting a coffee on the desk in front of me.

"Thanks," I say. "She told me you monster fucked her... Her words, not mine."

"Yeah... I did," he laughs. "Is that bad?"

"No. I'm glad you two have finally figured things out," I say.

"I hear you have had some shit going on," he says.

"Which one ran their mouth," I ask with a frown.

"Neither," he says. "What's going on?"

"Nothing I can't handle," I say. "You two have a meeting first thing at eight."

"Lorelei," he says.

"Cameron, please don't," I say with a sigh. I look up and see that Remy is standing in the doorway, leaning against the frame. "Can everyone just leave me alone?"

"Sorry. You are coming to the meeting you demanded to be a part of," Cam says to me with a smile. "Get your shit and come on."

"Whatever," I say. I grab my laptop and phone before standing. I go to step past Cam, but he stands and blocks me. "Cam..."

"Don't forget your coffee, sis," he says, handing me my cup. I frown at him before he finally moves. I get to the door, and Remy doesn't move.

"Move," I say. He just looks at me, studying me. "Goddamn it... Remy, please move."

"You and I need to talk later," he says simply, before stepping out of the way.

"Good fucking luck," I mutter. I walk out of the room and run into Tris.

"You ditched me," she frowns. I just step past her and go down to the conference room. They all follow, but it makes me just want to run. I am on edge and I can't stand it here today.

I get into the room and sit. Cam sits on one side of me and Remy is on the other. Tris sits beside Cam and I ignore them all and get on my laptop to start working. "Are you mad at me?" Remy asks softly as he leans in to speak.

"No."

"What's wrong?" he asks.

"Just feel like an idiot," I say simply. Cam starts the meeting, and I focus on typing out notes as they talk. I get lost in my thoughts and before I know it, I look up and everyone is staring at me.

"Does that work?" Cam asks.

"I was... sorry, does what work?"

"There is a meeting that one of us has to attend in Seattle. I have meetings here, so I am sending you with Remy," he says. "It's in two weeks. Does that work?"

"Uh... yeah," I say, making note of what he is saying. "I'll find reservations."

"Okay," he says to me before continuing with everyone else. I try to focus, but my thoughts keep drifting back to last night. I do my best to take notes, but the meeting is over and I have done nothing but sit here and stare at my computer.

As soon as people stand up and start to leave, so do I. I need to get out of this room before I implode. I grab my stuff, leaving my coffee, and rush back to my office. I kick the door open, even though both Remy and Cam have a key. I try to fill in the blank spots of memory of the meeting, but I fucked up. I'm fucking everything up.

"We need to talk," Cam says as he walks into my office. Remy is in the doorway but says nothing.

"What?" I snap.

"I think it's best that you go home," he says simply.

"Fine," I scoff and stand up. I pick up my bag and he steps in front of me. "Move."

"What has gotten into you, Lorelei?" he asks.

"A lot. That's the problem," I say vaguely, pointing toward my assumption that I am a whore.

"You didn't write a single note. You didn't hear a word anyone said. You have a massive attitude. What's wrong?" he asks.

"Am I fired?" I ask.

"No, Lori," he sighs.

"'Kay, I'll be here tomorrow then," I say as I push past him and go to the door.

"Lori," Remy says, glancing at Cam.

"Stop."

"You need to…"

"Move," I snap.

"Tell him or I will," he says simply.

"Fine," I say as I face my brother. "I worked in a strip club through college, but I never quit. I started letting men pay to fuck me. Friday night, a regular client brought friends and they hurt me. I tried to stop it, but there were three of them. I got myself raped because I'm a fucking idiot. One of them hit me, so that's why my eye is red. Makeup is covering the bruise he left. Happy? I can't get it out of my head. I can't stop thinking about it or the fact that I've ruined myself and now everyone deserves better than me, and there is nothing I can do to change it. There is nothing I can do to go back and convince myself to not cover up my pain by letting men use me."

I turn back to Remy and he steps out of my way. I take this opportunity to practically run away and get to the elevator. I manage to make it back to my car before bursting into tears. I'm so mad and sad all at once. I need to get out of my head. While still crying, I search for the studio near my apartment and call them. I take a deep breath and call to rent out the space.

I AM SITTING ON the floor with my back against one of the mirrors, staring at the pole. I rented the space every evening to make sure it's free for me to use when I want. After I talked to the owner, I went home and slept for a while before just watching television. I ended up turning my phone off because everyone kept calling me and I just don't feel like talking.

Now, it's late at night, and I can finally get out of my head. I have spandex shorts on and a sports bra so that it feels normal. I usually have next to nothing on, but they obviously require clothing. I tap on my phone to turn the music on and approach the pole.

Chapter Eight
Remington

"She still not answering?" Cam asks.

"No," I say. "I called the studio by her apartment and she signed the contract to rent it out today. She will probably be there tonight."

"I'm worried about her," he sighs.

"She's okay," Tris says.

"I don't know," Cam says.

"I do. She's embarrassed. That's it. She thinks she doesn't deserve Remy but then finds out he's saved himself for her. She feels like coping the way she did makes her unlovable but doesn't understand that Remy doesn't care who she's been with."

"Didn't know she remembered all of that," I say carefully.

"Did you really?" Cam asks me.

"Yeah…" I say.

"That's some wholesome shit," Cam says. "I can see how that scares her, though."

"Last night, when she was high, she said I just needed a good teacher," I chuckle.

"She is in love with you," Tris says. "Do you love her?"

"I do," I say.

"You should tell her that," Tris says.

"She isn't going to believe it," Cam says. "You'll have to do something drastic to get her attention."

"You mean like what you did to Tris?" I ask, raising an eyebrow.

"Yeah," he grins. "Go see her at the studio. See what she is like when she dances."

"She uses it as an escape, so it's much more than just stripping to her. That shit is an art," Tris says.

"I have an idea," I say as I stand. "I'm going to go."

"Steal her birth control and knock her up for me," Tris says, making Cam laugh.

I shake my head at her before saying my goodbyes. When I get to my car, I pull up her location.

A few months ago, I put a tracker in her. I'd like to say I'm not proud of that, but I am. It's wild how my mindset changes depending on my plans. Right now, I feel absolutely no regrets for what I have done with her. Maybe it's just because I know Lori and I know she won't be mad. I think she would be accepting of it. No matter what she has done prior, I think she trusts me on this level.

Instead of fighting the fact that the two sides of me are merging, I am going to throw it all at her at once. I don't care if I have to tie her to that bed and make her hear me out. By the time everything is said and done, she will be mine. I still won't fuck her until she knows and accepts. I'm a monster, but not that much of a monster. Is there a difference?

I get to her apartment and park my car before walking down to the studio. The back door is unlocked, so I slip inside. I hear the music, and my heart is thumping in my chest. I haven't had the luxury of seeing her dance before. I've wanted to see it for so long, and now is my chance.

When I get to her, I keep myself where she cannot see me. She is wearing shorts that may as well be panties and a sports bra that has her breasts practically popping out. She's alone, and she feels comfortable. Not only that, but she looks relaxed. I watch as she switches the song and sets her phone down before going back to the pole. I watch in awe as she gets herself on the pole and works herself upside down. She is spinning and twirling while keeping herself secure. She never slips or drops unless it's intentional.

I thought seeing her do this would be instantly arousing, but it's mesmerizing. She has an incredible strength to be able to keep herself up like that. Don't get me wrong, it's the sexiest thing I've ever seen anyone do, but it's because she is doing it. She flips off and lands in a split before rolling to lay on her back. She's breathing heavily, but she has a smile on her face. She's happy. This truly is her escape, and I feel lucky to be able to witness it.

She picks up her phone, and mine buzzes a second later.

Lori

> I'm okay. I just wanted you to know.

> I'm glad. Anything I can do?

> Tell me the truth.

> About?

> Everything. Your feelings for me mostly. I feel stupid for wanting you.

> Why, because I have no experience?

> No, because I have too much…

> You just have your master's in dick, is all. No judgment ;)

Lori

Smartass lol. You deserve someone who hasn't been run through.

> Why don't you let me worry about what I deserve and what I don't? You just focus on what lesson you'll teach me first.

Don't tease me. I'll fall off the pole from getting too wet.

> Mmmm. I've always been curious what it would be like to fuck a paralyzed girl.

That's awful!

> Ah, but you laughed, didn't you?

I did. I've got dark humor for days!

> What are you doing?

Going home. Don't worry. No tea or muscle relaxers tonight. I am going to raw dog sleep.

> I'm going to come by.

> Lori: is that a question?

> No. Just letting you know.

I put my phone away and slip out of the building so I can follow her. I think she senses me because she glances behind her and walks faster. By the time she gets to her building, I can feel her panic. What she doesn't know is that she is about to have to take the stairwell. What good is money if I can't pay people to shut an elevator down so I can run down and scare my little fawn in the stairwell?

One flight later, and she starts running up the stairs. I quicken my pace with her, and I can hear her little whimpers as she gasps for air. The moment she slows down from exhaustion, I grab her.

"Stop!" she starts to scream but I cover her mouth and hold her against the wall until she stops fighting.

"Run faster, Little Fawn," I growl in her ear. "You'll never be fast enough to escape what I'll do when I catch you."

I let go of her, and she darts up the stairs and runs faster. I take the stairs two at a time and keep pace right behind her. When she slows again, due to being tired, I simply smack her ass, and she continues. When she gets to her floor, she runs to her door and fumbles with her keys to try and get it open. As she slips her key into the lock, I put my hands on her waist. She freezes, but sighs in defeat.

"W-What do you want?" she asks with a shaky voice. She doesn't realize it's me, even though she has heard my voice already.

"Go inside, Little Fawn. Accept your punishment for running from me," I say.

Chapter Nine

Lorelei

I RELAX WHENEVER I realize that it's Remington. I have more questions than answers at this point, but I'm going to kick his ass for scaring me. Although, based on the way he had me pressed against the wall, I'm going to assume that he finds a certain level of enjoyment from my fear.

I unlock my door, and the second I step in, he picks me up and goes straight to my bedroom. I turn to find that he has a mask on. I know it's him, but I question it. I gasp loudly and start fighting him, but with very little effort, he nearly rips my clothes off as he gets me on my bed. Adrenaline is pumping through my veins and for whatever reason, I have tears in my eyes. He must think that I'm hurt. Something about the way he touches me sparks a memory in my brain that I wasn't aware was available. He's been here before.

"Wait, wait, wait," I say as he ties my wrists to my headboard. "Please. Please take off the mask. Remy, please."

He stops when he hears me say his name. He looks at me for a second but ultimately takes off the mask. The look on his face is unlike anything I've ever seen from him before. He is the same man, only darker. The sweet and innocent man is gone, and in its place is a slightly more unhinged version that is undoubtedly obsessed with me. He must be the man from the elevator that I see every night. Is this what he's been hiding? I knew that someone was following me home at night after the shift at the club, but I was sure it was Omar. I didn't have anything to back that up, but no one ever scared me, so I never did anything about it. I knew if it was a client that I would've been raped three times over by now, but they just walked with me. They stayed in the shadows, and no one ever fucked with me. It's like they were watching over me.

"You look scared," he remarks as he moves onto the bed between my legs.

"Not scared," I say. "Shocked."

"Oh?"

"How long have you been following me?" I ask.

"Longer than what is sane," he says simply.

"I always knew someone was there," I say. "I didn't know it was you, though."

"If you didn't know who it was, why not speak up?" he asks as he kisses my thigh.

"Because you were my guardian. You never spoke to me, you were just there," I sigh.

"You are reckless."

"You are crazy," I counter. He smiles wickedly at me before spreading my legs more and dropping his head to flick his tongue across my clit. "Oh, fuck."

"Tell me," he says, licking me again. "How many times do you think I've tasted your sweet little cunt?"

"Oh my God," I groan.

"Hmm?" he asks.

"I don't know," I say.

"I'm going to explain something, and then I'm going to eat your pussy until I think that you've had enough. Got it?"

"Yes! Okay. Yeah. I'm listening," I choke out.

"Every night, you put your kettle on the stove and go take a shower. Every night I put a sedative in your tea," he says. "Every night, I get to play with you."

"Just you?" I ask.

"What?" he asks, confused. "Yes. Just me."

"Okay," I say.

"I have done everything but fuck you in your sleep," he says. "I have forced my cock down your throat. I've made you come on my hand, but my favorite thing to do is to taste this sweet little pussy."

"You haven't..."

"I've never fucked you. The first time I have you on my cock, I want us both to be aware," he says.

"You're the man from the elevator," I choke out as he licks me again.

"What man?" he asks with a growl.

"T-There's a man... he's on the elevator every night. I usually see him on weekends. He doesn't say anything and I've never seen his face, but he's always there. That's you," I pant. "Why stalk me?"

"Because I like to see who you are when no one's watching," he says. "I like to see how you respond to me when you don't mean to."

"W-when was the first time you touched me?" I ask.

"You were almost nineteen," he says. "I've been watching you for far longer."

"Cam stalks Tris," I moan when he nips at my clit. "She doesn't know it, but I woke once when we were in the same dorm apartment."

"What did he do?"

"I think he was jerking off. I rolled over so I don't know," I say. "Please stop teasing me."

"Why do you think you are ruined?"

"Because I am. I've let men fuck me for years," I whine. "Remy."

"Whatever happened before now, I'm not concerned about it. Going forward, you belong to me. No one will ever touch you again. No one will ever feel you again. Understand?"

"Yes," I pant.

"Good girl," he says. I gasp when he latches onto my clit and sucks hard.

"Oh, God!" I moan loudly. My eyes roll back when he pushes two fingers into me and curls them in. I'm still sore, but he goes slowly.

"You see, Little Fawn, I know everything about your body. I know how to make you come, I know how to keep you on edge, I know how to make you soak this bed. I may have not been inside of you yet, but I know your body better than you," he brags.

"Then, for the love of God, make me come," I beg.

"Tell me one good thing about yourself," he says.

"What? Fuck. I don't know," I whine again. "I dance well."

"Good girl. Keep saying things and you'll get to come," he says as he starts lightly sucking on me. When he moves his fingers inside of me, I could cry.

"Ohhh, my God," I whimper. He starts to stop, so I yell something else. "I'm smart! I have a master's degree. Fuck, I wanna come…"

"One more," he mutters against me.

"Remy," I whimper. "I'm kind. I'm nice to everyone to a fault. Oh, my God!"

He finally sends me spiraling into an orgasm and doesn't let up. He is hitting every hidden spot inside me and playing me in ways I didn't know were possible. When he stops, I am gasping for air, trying to catch my breath. "Fuck," I choke out. He unties my wrists and brings me to his chest when he lies beside me. He has his body positioned to hide the fact that he's hard, but I know. He's never had someone take care of him before. He said that he has taken my mouth in my sleep, but he's never experienced someone giving it to him.

I should be mad. Shit, I should be furious at him. He did far more than just take advantage of me while I was sleeping. He drugged me and then played with me. Although I didn't necessarily consent, I never would've said no. Not to him, at least. I move up to my knees so I can face him, and he raises an eyebrow at me.

"What are you doing?" he asks.

"What I do best," I say as I unbutton his pants.

"Lori..."

"Nope. Be a good boy and shut the fuck up so I can suck your cock. You can have control back after you come for me," I say as I yank his jeans and boxers down. I try not to react when I see his dick, but holy fuck, he is huge. He attempts to stop me, but I grab hold of his cock and take him straight to the back of my throat.

"Oh fuck," he groans, fisting my hair. He doesn't force me and lets me lead. I put my hand on the bed beside him and use the other to stroke him as I bob up and down. "Oh, Lori. Dear God, woman."

Unlike him, I don't tease or edge him. I get him there and push him over the edge. When his body tenses and he groans deeply, I squeeze and massage his balls. "Fuck, Lori!" he moans. I keep him down my throat and swallow as he comes, but I don't stop. He is hypersensitive, and his body jerks when I don't stop. He finally pulls me off him, and I laugh as he brings me up. When I'm close enough, he grabs my face and kisses me hard.

"Good?" I ask when he has me lay my head on his chest. I hear his heart still beating fast in his chest and I laugh.

"For the record, I've gotten my dick sucked before but never like that," he says.

"You have?" I ask, looking up at him.

"I've done a lot of things, Lori. I've just never fucked anyone. I do love the enthusiasm though," he says with a grin.

"I should be mad at you," I say.

"You should." He gently strokes my hair and doesn't argue.

"I should be angry because you drugged me over and over again. You used me when I couldn't say no," I continue.

"I did and you should be," he says simply.

"Why did you do it?"

"I don't know." He is searching my face for the answer before continuing. "I've known for a long time that you are my forever. No matter how hard I tried to stay away and just leave you alone, I couldn't. You consume every thought in my mind, and I am calmest when I am next to you."

"That's... so fucking sweet in the most psychotic way," I say, and he laughs. "You deserve better than me, Remington."

"There's nothing better than perfect, Little Fawn. Your soul is home to me," he says sweetly.

"I love you," I say before I can talk myself out of it. "I've loved you for as long as I can remember. I've wanted you for years."

"I love you too, Lorelei," he says with a smile. "So fucking much."

"What now?" I ask before rolling to my back to look at the ceiling. "Where do we go from here?"

"Why were you upset today?" he asks.

"Because I felt embarrassed for throwing myself at you like a cheap hooker."

"If you hadn't of been high, I would have accepted your generous offer to teach me," he says as he rolls to me.

"What about now?" I ask.

"How do you feel?"

"Are you referring to the assault?" I ask, and he nods. "Your dick is giant, so it's going to be a little uncomfortable either way."

"What's my first lesson then, teacher?" He asks as he moves on top of me and settles between my legs.

"Women can't always go straight to fucking. Even if I want to, sometimes I need a little help getting there," I say.

"Foreplay," he says before kissing my neck.

"Yeah," I choke out. I sigh when he kisses his way down my chest before lightly sucking on my nipples. He rolls the other between his index finger and thumb. I gasp and arch my back to push my breasts out.

"How am I doing?" he asks, kissing me softly.

"I sense you've had lots of practice with foreplay," I say.

"Baby, I've had a lot of practice with your body too, but yes," he smirks. "Understand that this is the only time you will get to lead."

"I'll make it count." I smile.

"Are you going painfully slow to torture me?" he asks, narrowing his eyes.

"Kinda," I laugh. He grunts before leaning down to kiss me. I pull him down so I can wrap my arms around him, and he has his face buried in my neck. When he pushes the head of his cock into me, I gasp. He slowly sinks into me with a deep, guttural groan, and I suddenly can't catch my breath. He is stretching me, and my body struggles to fit him. I arch off the bed, gasping for air as I push him up. He moves up to his hands, and I get a tight hold on his biceps.

"Jesus, you are so fucking tight," he grunts.

"You're going to fucking break me, Remy," I whimper. "Please. Please. Go slowly."

When he starts to rock his hips to make slow thrusts, I groan deeply. "Teach me, Lori. Isn't that what you wanted?"

"You... Oh God, you're too big," I pant. He rolls and pulls me on top of him, letting me take over. I take all of him and sit up to try to get used to his size. I have my eyes closed and my hands on his chest. His hands are on my waist as I rock my hips. He is watching me try not to fall apart.

"Tell me what to do, Little Fawn. You look uncomfortable," he groans.

I bring myself down and kiss him. "Please, fuck me," I say.

"Be specific," he smirks. I realize that while he may be a virgin, he is no fool. He may have given me this moment, but he's about to fucking destroy me.

"Show me what you are hiding," I say. His smile is damn near evil before he pulls me down and wraps his arms around my chest. When he lifts his hips, I know I'm in trouble. He slams into me with so much force that I scream into his chest, and he doesn't stop.

Remy starts fucking me hard and fast, keeping me pinned against his chest while I scream my pleasures. Eventually he rolls us but leans up to flip me to my belly. I move up to my knees and keep my chest on the bed. I push my hips back, and I whimper each time I slam his cock into me. "Talk to me," he grunts.

"Hard, not fast," I gasp. "Oh fuck, Remy. Jesus, your cock is so big."

"Like this?" he asks, slowing his pace, but each thrust is punishingly hard.

"Yes! Oh God, yes," I cry out.

He shifts my hips, my knees are further apart, and my back dips deeper. His next thrust smashes against my G-spot and my breath catches. "That," I choke out. "Oh my God, just like that. Fuck, what are you doing to me?!"

I push my hips back, hinting at him to go faster. I severely underestimated his knowledge because he suddenly starts railing into me, hard and fast, and something primal takes over my brain. I grunt, growl, and moan as he pounds into me. His grunts turn to moans and soon, we are both spiraling hard into an orgasm together that leaves us both a breathless heap on the bed.

"Oh... my God," I pant. "What the fuck?"

"I feel like you are being a drama queen," Remy chuckles as he props up on his elbow to look at me.

"You.... The bed is soaked. I'm soaked. Do you realize what you did?" I ask.

"I do," he says with a smirk.

"I have never done that," I say.

"Ever?"

"No. I know it's possible, but no one has ever focused on me before. It's always been about them," I say.

"Lori, have you ever had sex outside of that club?" he asks, and I shake my head. "So, the first time you consensually had sex was there?"

"Yeah," I say.

"And you've never dated anyone?" he asks.

"No. You and Cam always scared them off," I laugh.

"Baby, you may have consented to what happened at the club, but that hardly counts," he says. "You've been fucked, but you've never fucked. Does that make sense?"

"Uh... yeah," I say. "I know how to please another man, though. Good for you."

"Baby, sex isn't just about me," he says. "It's about you and I connecting on the deepest level."

"Very... very deep level," I say with wide eyes. Remy laughs heartily and kisses me.

"Maybe we both have a little learning to do then," he says.

"Yeah," I say. "I guess so."

"You mentioned a man on the elevator," he says.

"Mhmm. That was you."

"No, Lori. That wasn't me," he says carefully.

"What?" I ask, sitting up. He sits up with me and looks serious. "It has to be."

"No, baby. I used the fire escape. What did he look like?"

"Uh... He always has a hood on and would never let me see his face. He smells... familiar. I can't explain it," I say. "He is tall, but hunches over a little, so I don't know how tall."

"Hmm. Okay," he says. "I want you to come stay with me."

"You sure?"

"Yeah. We can set you up a space in the basement to dance, but keep your time reserved at the studio, so you have somewhere if you need to escape," he says. "I don't love that the elevator guy was hiding his face, though. How long ago did he start showing up?"

"Uh... probably about six months ago was when I first noticed him," I say. "Was it you that followed me home?"

"Yeah," he says. "I wouldn't go inside, though. I would just go around the building to the fire escape. It's better hidden over there."

"You are crazy, you know that?" I ask. "Like... You hid that well."

"You don't seem too offended, Lori. What does that say about you?"

"That crazy attracts crazy." I grin. "Are you going to tell Cam about-"

I don't get the words out of my mouth before I hear my brother's voice. "Cam already knows, but now I'm traumatized too," he says from the doorway. I scream and pull the blanket over my head, curling up in a ball, making Cam, Remy, and Tris laugh at my reaction.

"Come out from under there," Remy chuckles and tries to pull the blanket away.

"No," I say, holding tight on the covers. He pulls it down just enough so he can see my face and kisses the end of my nose. "I'm naked."

"Child, sit up here and put a shirt on," Cam says.

"Don't call her a child. If she is a child, I'm a predator," Remy says.

"You are a predator, dipshit," Cam laughs, making me giggle. "Lorelei, sit up, or I'll tickle you."

"No, you..." I start to say but squeal and wiggle away when he tickles my side. "Fine. Rude ass."

"Put a shirt on," he says, tossing me a shirt. Once I have it on, he sits in front of me and stares at Remy.

"Cam," I say. "If I'm not mad, you can't be."

"She has a point," Tris says. "Also... I kinda... might have known."

"What?" Remy and I ask.

"So... I came by super late one night before your birthday," Tris says, and Remy laughs.

"I wanna know, but Cam looks like he might get violent," I say.

"Did you ever touch her before she was eighteen?" Cam asks Remy.

"No, Cameron," Remy says. "She was in college."

"Why?" he asks.

"Cameron," I say.

"What?" he asks, not looking at me.

"Does Beatris know?" I ask, and he looks at me. "Maybe make sure your little sister is actually asleep before you go jerk off to her best friend in the same room."

"Ha. I told you she knew," Tris laughs.

"I never put a fucking tracker in her," Cam counters.

"No, but you touched her. Right?" I ask, and he stays silent. "Right?"

"Yes," Cam finally answers.

"So, you are both creeps," I say. "Turns out Tris is just as insane as me."

"A tracker, Lori?" he complains.

"That tracker is no different to you hacking my fucking phone and watching my location," I say, and he smiles. "You knew I worked at the club, didn't you?"

"I did," he says.

"Which of you killed George and the other two idiots?" I ask.

"Oh, that was me," Remy says.

"And there is no way it can come back on you?" I ask.

"No," he says confidently.

"How?" Cam asks.

"Wooden bat," Remy shrugs.

"Fuck yeah," Cam says, fist bumping him. "So, what's this about some other guy following you?"

"He's just in my elevator," I say. "I figured he lived here."

"Maybe he does," Tris shrugs.

"Why are you here?" I ask Cam.

"Well, I wanted to see if you were okay," he says. "Remy said he had an idea but never texted back when we checked in, so we came here."

"How much of that..." I start to ask.

"We walked in pretty early on, but I didn't want to interrupt, and Tris didn't want to leave," he says.

"He covered his ears like a baby," Tris laughs.

"Joking aside," Cam says. "I can handle it; I just don't want to see it. Next time, we will knock louder."

"It's late." I yawn.

"Well, we will sleep on the couch. You two get some rest," Cam says. "We can split up in the morning and get what we need for work."

"There isn't anything planned until the quarterly meeting at eleven," I say.

"Yeah, so we can afford to be late," Remy adds as he lays me down.

"Night," I sigh and snuggle up to Remy when he lies down with me.

"Night," Cam says. When it's just us again and my bedroom door is shut, Remy lifts my chin.

"Are you happy?" he asks.

"I am. Why do you ask?"

"You don't have to be okay with what I did, Lorelei," he says. "I am no better than the…"

"Stop," I cut him off. "You and I both know that I would have been consenting either way with you. I truly don't think you would have if you had known I wouldn't be interested... You are not them. I am not your victim."

"You are, Lori," he pushes.

"Okay. So, if I am okay with it with you, then I have to accept what George did. Right?" I ask. "If I am your victim, you deserve the same treatment that you gave them for doing what they did to me."

"I didn't hurt you," he says with a frown. "That's not the same."

"At least they gave me a chance to say no," I say.

"Lori," he says with a sad tone.

"Why are you defensive if you already think you are guilty?" I ask. "This is what you want, right? You want me to blame you... Call you a monster?"

"I get it," he says with a sigh as he rolls to his back.

"Fuck no. You are not getting out of this that easily," I say as I sit up. He goes to sit up with me, but I move to straddle his body while he is still naked, and I don't have panties on. He groans and rubs his hands down his face, but I grab his wrists and lay his hands on my thighs. "I am the only one who gets to decide what hurts and what doesn't. Not you. Not Cam. Not Tris. If I had a problem with what you did, it wouldn't take much to get Cam to handle it. When those men hurt me, I may have not fought them, but I spoke up. Not everyone has that ability, but I do. I did it as a teen, and I am doing it now."

"I understand, Lorelei," he says simply.

"You're just saying that so I'll shut up," I say with a frown. I yelp when he grabs me by the throat and pulls me down for a kiss. I relax and move my hands to the bed to support myself.

"I'm conflicted because I know I should feel bad, but I don't," he explains. "I knew you'd be consenting, but I still took advantage of you. That should eat me alive, but it doesn't. That makes me no better than the men who hurt you in that room."

"Those men," I say as I shift my hips and slowly lower onto his cock, filling myself inch by inch. "Only cared about their pleasure. Not mine. Theirs. They didn't take the time to get me off... No, they fucked me and found pleasure in my pain. Does the thought of me sobbing while you fuck me make you want to fuck me harder?"

"No," he groans.

"Then just shut the fuck up about it and do what you did to me all of those times you came into this room and played with me while I slept," I say, slowly moving my hips.

"Fuck, Lori," he groans. "I'm going to kick your little ass for topping."

"Do it, Remington. Where is that man who throat-fucked me in my sleep?" I ask. "Hmm?"

"I can't. Cam is here..."

"Well then, you better learn how to get me to shut the fuck up or I am not stopping," I warn. "I will fucking edge you until you break."

"Why, Lori?" he groans. I can see it on his face that he wants to.

"You tore yourself in half, Remy. Part of you, everyone else saw, but the other side hid in this room with me while I slept. I want to meet him. I want to meet the man who claims to own me," I say. I tighten my pussy around his cock, and his eyes roll back. I take all of him and stay seated on him. "You have two fucking choices here, Remy. You can either let me see the real you, or I'm in charge. You come when I tell you to come. You get on your fucking knees for me when I tell you to. If you don't want to dominate me, then I will happily take you down a few fucking notches. You think I am above tying you to this bed and making you come so many times that you beg me to stop? Eventually, you'll come dry and there wouldn't be a goddamn thing you can do about it. How hard do you think you'll come for me when I have your cock in a sucking machine while I fuck your ass with a dildo cast from your dick? Please... try me. See how fucking far that will get you. I live to make grown men cry and you are not a fucking exception."

Remy's eyes are darkened, and his teeth are gritted. He's pissed off and seconds from breaking. I want to draw out the side of him that spent all of that time with me. I know Remy, but I want to meet my guardian.

"Have it your way," I laugh. I start to move off him, and he breaks.

All of a sudden, Remy flips us. He lays his hand over my mouth and slams into me so hard that a scream rips from my throat, but he doesn't stop. After a second, he brings my legs to his shoulders and leans into me so he can wrap his hands around my throat as he pounds into me. I can't breathe, but he doesn't give a fuck. I wanted to meet this side, and now I am. Every minute or so, he lets me breathe, but he never slows down or gives me any reprieve from fucking me hard and deep.

"You are my fucking toy to break, Little Fawn," he growls. "Mine. I fucking own you, this cunt, and every fucking breath you take. You wanted this so badly, well here the fuck I am, baby. You will never escape me; not even in death."

It feels as though he is fucking the soul out of my body. Everything feels like one giant orgasm. My body is tense and I am shaking violently as my arousal floods out of me every time I come.

"Oh my God," I choke out when he abruptly stops without coming and uncovers my mouth.

"Don't forget you asked for this, Lori," he says as he pulls my arms up and ties them to the headboard with his belt. With one knee beside my head, his other foot flat on the bed and his hands fisting my hair, he shoves his cock down my throat.

This man starts throat-fucking me far faster than anyone has ever done to me. I, for whatever reason, start fighting and thrashing under him, but it only makes him groan and go faster, deeper. When I get myself to stop fighting, I suck hard. Remy lets out a delicious moan from deep in his chest, and I can feel how his cock pulsates in my throat as he starts to fall.

"Fuuuuck, yes. Swallow me... Fuck, just like that. Good girl. Yes," he moans.

"Well damn, Remy," I pant. He unties my arms before leaning down to get in my face.

"The next time you try to top me, I'm taking your ass. No mercy. No holding back. You want to be a bratty little shit, fine. You want to meet the man in me that should fucking terrify you, *fine*. You've got no goddamn idea what you've released, Lori," he growls in my face.

"I've set you free," I say with a soft smile. "You don't have to hide who you are with me anymore."

Instead of responding, he kisses me and brings himself down to lay his head on my chest. I can feel it in his body that he needs comfort, but has no idea how to ask for it. Has anyone ever comforted this man? Something tells me that he is just as broken as I am. I pull him up so I can lay his head between my breasts and gently run my fingers through his hair. He slides his hand up my shirt and cups my breast and relaxes into me. I have tears rolling down my face as I realize that someone has hurt him badly for him to be this broken.

When his breathing evens out, and he falls asleep in my arms, I manage to get the blanket over our lower half just as Cam peeks his head in. I am trying to sniff back my tears so my crying doesn't wake Remy, but it fucking hurts to know I can't take away his pain.

"Hey, I thought I heard your sniffling," Cam says softly. He sits beside me and looks at Remy for a moment.

"Someone hurt him," I say quietly.

"Did he tell you?"

"No," I say. "I just know. I can recognize brokenness, because I am just as broken. Who hurt him?"

"His mom," Cam says.

"Maggie?" I ask, shocked, and he nods. "From the time he was about twelve until he was sixteen, she raped and beat him. He had bruises, but they stayed hidden by clothing."

"You were over there a lot..."

"I was," he says, watching my face.

"She hurt you too, didn't she?"

"Yeah. She'd drug him every night practically. He was aware, but too weak to move. She'd ride him and just repeatedly make him come. She said it was to teach him how to be a better lover."

"That's fucking awful," I say. "Did she…"

"I made the decision to stay with him as much as I could so that he wasn't alone," he explains. "When I was there, I got the same treatment. I was groggy, but I remember most of it. I remember once when I was sixteen… She focused on him for so long that he passed out. She got to me, and the drugs were wearing off."

"Uh oh…"

"Mmm. Yeah, uh-oh for her," he says. "When she got on top of me, I snapped. I grabbed her by the hair and slung her down to the bed. He woke up about the time I put her face in a pillow and fucked her ass while she screamed and begged for mercy. I was fucking her dry, and I was fueled by rage and whatever the fuck she gave us. She bled and sobbed, but I didn't stop. Eventually I switched and fucked her vaginally, and again… I didn't stop. I was so fucking angry for him. I didn't care that she hurt me too because I know it brought him comfort to not be alone anymore… When I finished, I flipped her over and got in her face. I told her if she ever touched him again, I'd fucking kill her. I told her she was going to sign the paper to let him start college with me, since we graduated early, and she'd never speak to him again… I cleaned up, packed his shit, and brought him to the house. The next day, she signed the papers, and we started college a month later."

"Jesus…" I say.

"He has never spoken about it since and he's not seen her since that night," Cam adds. "He found a lot of comfort in you, and I knew a long time ago that someday you two would be together… When you were raped in high school, it hurt him a lot. I think that's when he really got attached to you."

"Is that why he did the things to me that he did?" I ask.

"I don't know what specifically he did to you," he says.

"From what I am gathering, he would drug my tea at night and wait until I fell asleep. He sometimes would get himself off by hand or orally, but he mostly just got me off, I think. I know he never fucked me," I say.

"All he ever knew was abuse," Cam says. "I'm not saying what he did was right because I did the same shit to Tris. Hell, I am probably more traumatized by that than I realized until you called me out for it. Remy is a good guy with a good heart. I think the two of you can heal together."

"So… I was trying to get him to break and show me the part of him that he was when he would visit me at night… I might have threatened to tie him down and make him come without mercy," I say, and Cam chuckles.

"How'd that go for you?"

"Uh… Violently," I smile. "I got what I wanted and deserved."

"I am guessing you think you triggered him?"

"He looked mad…"

"Honey, you are a brat. A giant one," Cam says. "I know my best friend, and I know my little sister. You push and push until you get what you want, but it's never unreasonable. It's never for your benefit, either. If you had triggered him, he wouldn't have fucked you; he would have told you. Remington has a voice, just like you do. Have faith that if you cross a line, he will speak up."

"I love him… so much, Cam," I say.

"I know you do," Cam says. "I told Mom and Dad, by the way."

"Oh?" I ask. "What did they say?"

"Mom cried. Dad was pretty quiet. I asked their thoughts, and they said they didn't care that you were working at the club or even that you consented to doing extra. They were more so just upset you got hurt… I told them you quit, and they were happy about that."

"So, they aren't disappointed?"

"No, Lorelei," he says. "No one is or ever has been disappointed in you."

"Good," I sigh. "He's holding my boob, and it's low-key adorable."

"Boobs are comforting," Cam shrugs. "You should get some sleep."

"Yeah," I say. "Thank you for checking on me."

"You are welcome," he says. "Please don't fuck in my office. Keep it to yours."

"We'll see," I say with a grin. "Goodnight, Cam."

"Night, sis," he laughs as he leaves the room and shuts the door.

"We can fight our demons together, Remy," I say, kissing the top of his head and closing my eyes. "We never have to be alone again."

Remy doesn't say anything, but I know he was awake for most of that. He simply slides his arm under my back so he can squeeze my body against his. He settles again, and this time, we both drift off to sleep.

Chapter Ten
Lorelei

I AM SITTING AT my desk typing when my office door comes open. I glance up and smile when I see that it's Remy. "Hey. I am almost done," I say as I resume typing. He walks around behind me to look at my screen, resting his hands on my shoulders.

"How long have you been sitting here typing?" he asks as he starts to knead my shoulders.

"Oh, that's nice," I sigh and slow down. "I'm so close, Remy. Please let me finish."

"Go on. I'm not stopping you," he says, working my tired muscles. I fight through the final few lines before dropping my head and pushing my keyboard away. Remy chuckles and presses in on the knots in my neck, making me groan.

"It sounds like you are getting fucked in here," Cam says from my doorway.

"Shh," I say, shooing him away.

"Meeting is in five," Cam laughs. Remy leans down and kisses my shoulder, and I whine when he stops massaging my neck.

"Come on. I can massage your back when we get home," Remy says.

"My home or yours?" I ask.

"Our home, and your things are being moved over today," Remy says as I stand.

"Wait. What?" I ask, turning to him.

"Uh oh," Cam laughs.

"Why?" I ask.

"Because I know you," Remy says. "You'll never willingly take that step because you'll think you are intruding, which you aren't considering I'm now making you move in with me."

"Oh," I say. "Well... Okay."

"Ready?" he asks, kissing me.

"Uh," I say, turning around to grab my laptop and phone. "Yep."

I walk with Remy and Cam to the conference room. Tris is already here, but we are still missing a few clients and board members. This meeting happens four times a year. It is essentially a time for everyone related to the company to get together and give one giant update. It lasts hours, so I am going to be typing a lot of notes today. I am also going to be covering a few of our updates, but I already have everything typed out for us. I'll just have to add in any commentary from others if it seems notable.

I am getting everything set up when I hear more people come into the room. "We will get started in just a few minutes, everyone," Cam says. "Ready, Lorelei?"

"Yes," I say. I glance up but do a double take when a man across the large table is staring me down. He leans back in his seat with a smirk on his lips. I know him... but how?

"Oh fuck," I say. A few people look over, and I get glared at by both Cam and Remy, but they both instantly flip back to brother and boyfriend, rather than my bosses, when they see the panicked look on my face.

"What's wrong?" Cam asks softly, but I don't answer. Everyone else is lost in their own world, but this man... Matthew Hernandez... He is staring me down just like he did in that club. Just like he did every time he sat in the front and watched me before eventually ending up in one of the back rooms.

"Lori," Remy says, making me look at him.

"Everything okay?" Tris asks as she comes over and squats down.

"Why is Matthew Hernandez here?" I ask softly.

"He is a new client," Cam says. "Why? Do you know him?"

"He… He came into the club maybe twice a month," I say.

"Fuck," Remy sighs.

"It's no big deal," Cam says to me. "We will talk to him after. Okay?"

"He's paid me, Cam," I say, ready to burst into tears. "Since I first started there."

"Just breathe," Cam says. "Whatever happens, we can fix it. Okay?"

"If the media…"

"Then we will stand by your side and defend you no matter what," he says. "Okay?"

"Okay," I whisper.

We turn back to the table, and Tris moves her things down to sit with us. Matthew is still looking at me. "Want me to give the update?" Remy asks.

"No, it's fine," I sigh.

"Okay," Remy says before turning to everyone else. "Lorelei is going to give some basic updates before we get into our quarterly plan."

"Who is she?" Matthew asks simply.

"She is my younger sister and Remington's partner. She is our COO and handles all administrative dealings," Cam says, and Matthew nods.

"Just wondering. She's not been in meetings before," he says.

"She has always been privy to the meetings. We've just adjusted her schedule so she can attend," Cam adds before looking at me.

The conference room hums with the quiet murmur of anticipation as I stand at the head of the long, polished table. Every pair of eyes is on me, and I take a deep breath and pick up the remote to the projector. I am forcing myself to not look at Matthew; otherwise, I will meltdown in front of everyone.

"Good morning, everyone. Let's dive straight into the numbers," I say, clicking the remote in my hand. The first slide appears, and their eyes shift from me to the screen. "We have once again exceeded expectations this quarter. Our revenue for quarter three hit $2.3 billion, which is a 15% increase compared to the previous quarter. This marks our sixth consecutive quarter of growth."

I glance at Cam, and he nods, telling me to keep going. "The growth was driven by the remarkable performance of our Sentinel line of cybersecurity products. We saw a 22% growth in subscriptions, largely fueled by our new AI-driven threat detection module. Early adopters are already reporting a 35% decrease in security breaches, which translates into strong retention and positive feedback."

I click to the next slide, showing a chart that highlights the rise in customer satisfaction scores. "Speaking of feedback, our Net Promoter Score has jumped to seventy-eight, the highest it's been in company history... On the innovation front, we're gearing up to launch the beta for PinnacleOS, which we anticipate will revolutionize cloud integration for mid-size enterprises. Pre-launch interest is already double what we projected, so we're entering the next quarter with strong momentum."

I click the remote, and it brings up my portion of the updates. "On the administrative side, I want to share some updates to keep everything transparent. Our employee turnover has dropped to 8%, which is down from 12% last quarter, which started changing after we revamped our retention initiatives as far as benefits, insurance, incentives, vacation and sick time pay, and general office activities that allow everyone to bond and get to know management better. The new mentorship program has received overwhelmingly positive feedback, with over 70% of participants noting improved engagement and career satisfaction. Additionally, our hybrid work model continues to thrive as it allows us to cater to the employees with children. We noticed a trend that when employees went on maternity leave their feedback, when they would ultimately quit, indicated concerns surrounding childcare. Allowing them to work from home meant that we were able to retain them as employees, and they didn't have to search for something new to accommodate their home life.

"On the topic of home life, over 85% of employees surveyed reported increased productivity and work-life balance under the new structure. We're also proud to announce that our DEI efforts have led to a 20% increase in diverse hires across all levels of the company. Lastly, our investments in upskilling have yielded measurable results, as over 60% of employees have completed advanced training certifications so far this year. We do have incentives in place for those who complete the training before its ultimate due date, and it results in minimal lapses of certifications."

"Thank you for that," Cam says. "Does anyone have any questions?"

"Were the numbers driven up by the efforts of the employees... or the actions of upper management?" Matthew asks, his eye shifting from Cam to me and then back to Cam.

"Every person involved has helped shaped this company and influence the growth that we are seeing," Cam says simply. "Without our employees, we simply would not be where we are today."

"So, you're not partnered with any other entities that would allow for easier growth?" he pushes.

Fuck... He is suggesting that I am fucking people to help the company grow.

"No," Remy says coldly, understanding. "I think that covers our updates. Cameron?"

For the remainder of the meeting, I focus entirely on listening and taking notes. I don't look up because I don't want to get distracted. I can feel him watching me, even when he gives his own update. It's not until Cam ends the meeting that I look up.

"You did well. Good job," Cam says as people file out of the room.

"Thanks," I say. I glance over and see that Matthew hasn't moved. "He's going to bring it up. This is bad."

"Just breathe," Cam says. "I promise, we have your back, no matter what."

When there is no one left but us and Matthew, he finally speaks. "I must say, Ms. Belmont. You look much different with clothes on," Matthew says.

"What do you want, Matthew?" I ask. "That's why you are still here, right? Get something for nothing?"

"Nothing? You think others won't see the connection between this company and you fucking business executives for money in an exclusive strip club?" he asks.

"What do you want?" Cam asks. "Are you trying to tattle on her, or do you have a legitimate concern?"

"You see, I feel as though I was forced into a sexual interaction with Ms. Belmont in order to secure a contract between my company and Saltz-Belmont Technologies," he says with a smirk.

"That's bullshit, and you know it," I snap. "You knew the entire fucking time who I was, didn't you? If anything, I should be the one to have an issue with your creepy ass following me around like a lost puppy when you came in."

"Oh, I came alright," he says. "Over. And over. And over. You remember, right?"

"Is this necessary?" Remy asks.

"How do you feel knowing your girlfriend has done what she has?" Matthew asks. "Will you visit her in jail when she gets charged with soliciting?"

"What do you want?" Cam asks. "Money, right? How much?"

"Ten million," he says seriously, and I laugh.

"You've lost your goddamn mind," I say. "No."

Matthew taps on his phone before sounds play through the room. When he turns the screen around, it's me on stage. I can feel all the color drain from my face as he goes to the next, and it's of a private room. "One hour or it goes to the press," he says as he stands.

"Go ahead," Cam says with a shrug.

"Cameron," I snap, but he ignores me.

"Suit yourself," Matthew says with a matching shrug. "By the way, Remington. You're lucky. The girl can suck a cock better than any whore I've ever met."

"Get the fuck out of my building," Cam says with a grave tone.

"Ah, but we have a contract. I'll see you next week, everyone," he smiles before leaving the room. I stand from my chair to get away from them as I start to hyperventilate.

"Hey. Hey. Hey," Tris says, holding my face. "You're okay. The company will be fine. We will be fine. You will be fine. Okay? The media will hyper-focus. You'll have to explain things in a bit, but…"

"Rob will get in trouble," I whimper. "He never hurt me. He shouldn't get in trouble. He kept us safe."

"Let's go see him then, huh? The club is open, right?"

"Yeah," I sniff.

"Let's go see him so he will at least have a heads-up," she says. "Guys?"

"Yeah. Let's go," Cam says. "I promise, we will get through this, sis."

"Easy for you to say," I say coldly. "You aren't the one who is about to be publicly slut-shamed or blamed for this entire company going to shit."

"Lorelei, we will stand beside you no matter what," Cam says. "Surely you accounted for someone finding out one day."

"I mean, I did. I just assumed that none of them would speak up as they would out themselves also," I say. "Let's just warn Rob and... I don't know. I don't know what to do."

We walk into the club and Omar is up front. "Hey, girl," he smiles, hugging me tightly. "Who are they? You okay?"

"Oh, uh. This is my brother Cameron, my best friend and his girlfriend, Beatris, and my... boyfriend, Remington. He's also Cameron's best friend," I say. "This is Omar."

"Nice to meet you guys," Omar says. "What brings you here?"

"Is Rob around?" I ask.

"Yeah. He's in his office. Is everything okay?"

"Uh... no," I say.

"Well, go on back," he says.

"Probably... shouldn't open," I say. "Let me talk to Rob first."

"Uh oh," Omar says. "Okay."

I wave the others back with me, and we walk on to the main floor. Some of the girls are out and wave at me as I walk back to Rob's office. I knock and hear him answer right away. "It's okay," he says.

"Hey, Rob," I say.

"Hey, Lorelei," he smiles, but his face drops when he sees Remy. "What's wrong?"

"You know each other?" I ask Remy.

"Yeah," he smirks.

"Okay… I feel like that deserves an explanation," I say.

"Oh, he was just looking out for you. Never had many issues, so there was no need to tell him much," Rob says. "What's going on?"

"Matthew Hernandez," I say.

"Oh God. Him," Rob says, rolling his eyes. "What did he do?"

"He is a client of the company, apparently," I say. "He attended the quarterly meeting today and… He knew who I was the whole time. He basically said that if we didn't give him ten million, that he was going to go to the media. He gave us an hour and that was forty minutes ago."

"Oh hell," Rob says.

"He has video, Rob. Of me. Of the back rooms," I say. "Every single client…"

"Fuck," Rob snaps. "Come on. Let's tell the girls."

We follow Rob out to the main floor, and he calls all the girls out. "So many boobs," Tris says.

"You'll get that in a strip club," I laugh.

"Okay girls…" Rob sighs. He tells them what I told him, and they all listen without interrupting. All of them look sad, but a few look like they're mad.

"So, what now?" Angel asks. "Are we going to jail now?"

"No," Rob says.

"Don't lie to them," I say.

"Girls… I knew that this was a possibility. None of you have done anything wrong. I've always believed that you should be able to do whatever you want with your body, so I've kept you safe and allowed you to do what you want… I've never forced any of you ladies to do anything. You aren't a hostage," he says.

"Rob. No. Absolutely not," I say, but he ignores me.

"When the police show up… Tell them I made you. The only way you get out of this without getting in trouble is if they think that I trafficked to you," he says as he gets emotional.

"Rob, you can't just..." Dazzle starts to say.

"Girl, stop. I know you don't want to do this. I know it feels wrong, but I'm not letting you all get in trouble," he says. "I'll destroy my records and... Well, just lie. Just get your story straight."

"Rob," I say tearfully. He walks over and hugs me.

"Lorelei, honey. I can't let you get in trouble for this. I can't," he says. "Tell them I made you do it and I took half. You were too scared to speak up."

"Are you sure about this?" Cam asks.

"Absolutely," Rob confirms. "I don't have a wife or kids. It's just me. I'm not leaving anybody behind."

"I'll make some calls and make sure you have a good lawyer if this is what you really want," Remy says. "Thank you for looking after them."

"I did everything I could to keep them safe and let them do what they wanted. No one should have the right to tell these girls what they can and can't do with their bodies. All the clients treated them right, and we hardly ever had issues. When we did, it was handled," Rob says. "I'll throw myself under the bus to make sure they don't get in trouble."

"Uh... Lori," Tris says slowly. "He didn't wait an hour."

"What?" I snap, turning to her. She handed me her phone, and I see the video.

"It's everywhere," she says sadly. "It's been up for less than five minutes, and it's already like five hundred thousand views."

"Was she named?" Cam asks.

"Yeah," she says. She plays a breaking news story from the media, and everyone is silent as they listen.

"...Breaking news. Lorelei Belmont, COO of Saltz-Belmont Technologies, has been seen in a recent video as an adult entertainer at a local club here in New York City. There are reports coming in that she was soliciting sex for money. One source says that the business owners, Cameron Belmont and Remington Saltz, were using Lorelei to blackmail other executives into business dealings for the technology company. We will have more information as it becomes available..."

"Y'all need to get out of here before the cops show up," Rob says. "Girls, go about your business, but do not take any clients to the back rooms. Understand?"

"Rob," I say tearfully.

"It's okay, Lorelei," he says as he hugs me. "You girls are like my kids. Let me protect you. Okay?"

"You'll go to jail, Rob. Forever. Human trafficking is a huge charge," I sniff.

"I know, hun. I know," he says. "I'll do what needs to be done to make sure none of you gets dragged into this. You all have bright futures ahead of you. I'm just an old man."

"We should go," Remy says softly to me.

"Go on, Miss Lolita," Rob smiles, his eyes full of unshed tears. Remy takes my hand and pulls me along. Omar stops us to hug me.

"You'll be okay, girl," Omar says.

"Omar, I love you, son. Get the fuck out of here," Rob says. "Go home and don't get caught up in this. I have files to delete."

"Cops," Dazzle calls out, looking at her phone. "My man said there is a group of them driving this way."

"Come on," Remy says, pulling me out.

We all run outside and get back to the car. I am in tears by the time we are pulling out of the parking lot. I'm sitting in the backseat with Remy while Cam drives. A few seconds after we pull out and driving down the road, we see a pack of police cars pull into the parking lot of the club.

"I'm sorry, Lori," Remy murmurs as he holds me in his lap.

Chapter Eleven

Lorelei

WE'VE BEEN WATCHING THE news, waiting for the cops to show up. Cameron expressed that we would make a statement in the morning, and were taking the evening to process things. Mom and Dad are here with us, and we are all sitting in the living room of Remington's house. It's the only property between all of us that is gated, so it will keep people away from me. It's not stopping them from being at the gate, though.

I am curled up in Remy's lap when Cam sighs. "Cops at the gate," he says.

"I'm going to jail," I say tearfully.

"No, you're not," Dad says as he sits on the ottoman in front of me. "Look at me."

"I'm sorry, Daddy," I say as I choke back tears. I sit up and face him, letting him take my hands.

"I will never judge you for the things that you decide to do. Your mother and I love you no matter what, you understand that, right?"

"Yes," I sniff.

"Rob Lasson was arrested and is being charged with fifteen counts of human trafficking. They officially arrested him about an hour ago," Dad says gently. "None of the girls were arrested."

"I don't want to lie," I say.

"Baby, you have to," Dad says. "If you go against what the other girls said, you'll all go to jail."

"Okay," I sniff. There is a knock at the door, and Cam answers it.

"I am Detective Ross Yotes. Is Lorelei here?" he asks.

"Yeah," Cam says, stepping out of the way. The man walks in and I don't look up at him as my dad moves to the other couch.

"I am Detective..."

"I heard," I say.

"Then you know why I am here," he says.

"Because of the club," I say quietly.

"Yes, ma'am. Can you tell me about your boss, Rob?" he asks.

"He, uh…" I say as I start to cry. I don't want to lie, even if he wants me to. "I didn't have a choice…"

"He made you take clients to the back room?" Defective Yotes asks, and I nod as tears roll down my cheeks. "What about the claims of blackmail?"

"Cameron and Remington didn't know about any of that until now," I say, wiping my face. "No one ever blackmailed anyone. Matthew Hernandez tried to blackmail me, though. He wanted ten million to not say anything."

"So, he pursued you?" he asks, and I nod.

"Am I in trouble?"

"No. Mr. Lasson has admitted to this and the other girls at the club, too," he says.

"Then why are you here?" I ask with a frown.

"Just doing the due diligence of checking in with you, considering everything going on in the media," he says. "Tell me about your time there."

"Is this necessary?" Dad asks? "She's been through enough as it is."

"I'll just ask this then," the detective says. "Did Rob Lasson ever rape you or force you to do anything of a sexual nature with him?"

"No," I say quietly.

"Okay," he says. "Here in a few days, we need to sit down and do a full statement. Okay?"

"She'll be there," Dad says simply.

"If you need anything in the meantime…"

"I have my family," I interrupt. He nods and looks at me for a moment. "Remy, I'm exhausted. Can we go to bed?"

"Yeah, sweetie," Remy says, softly kissing me. "Go on up, and I'll see them out. I'll bring us up something to eat."

"Okay," I say before looking at my family. "Thank you all for coming. Truly… Your support means so much."

"Of course," Cam says. "Tris and I will come over in the morning, and we can all ride together."

"Are you planning on making a statement in the morning?" the detective asks Cam and Remy.

"We are. We wanted to have the evening to let her relax before we have to deal with everything at the office," Remy says.

"I will come as well, so we can make sure she is safe. It is unknown if he was working for anyone," the detective says.

"Night, everyone," I say.

I all but run away, trying to escape. Trying to breathe. I get upstairs and go to the master bedroom. I've been here so many times, so I know where everything is. I go to the bathroom and strip off my clothes after turning the shower on. I close my eyes and focus on breathing. When the water is scalding hot, I step in, and it takes my breath away as it burns my skin.

I am nearly panting, trying to breathe through the searing pain. It makes me feel more alive than anything else ever has. I don't know why I do this, but it is so goddamn soothing.

"Woah. None of that," Remy says as he suddenly flips the water to cold. I try to escape, but he wraps his arms around my body and forces me to stay under the water as it turns ice cold.

"Stop," I yell at him. "It's cold. Remy!"

"Shhh. Breathe with me, Little Fawn," he murmurs, holding me against his chest. I am gasping for air, trying to force oxygen back into my lungs after the frigid water stole it. "There you go. Good girl. Just breathe." It takes me way too long to realize that I am hysterically crying. How long have I been sobbing? I was so out of it, standing under the hot water. When I calm down, he shuts the water off and lets me turn to hug him.

"I'm sorry," I sniffle.

"You have done nothing wrong, Lorelei," he says, lifting my chin.

"But the company…"

"I don't give a fuck about the company, baby. I care about you. We will stand by your side while that place crumbles behind us," he says softly.

"I'm scared," I admit.

"We will do the talking. Don't hold back any emotion; just stand with us and we will handle the rest," he says.

"What about Matthew?" I ask.

"You keep your head held high, and you do your job. You are damn good at what you do, so just focus on that," he says. "Nothing will change. You will keep the same responsibilities."

"What about the board?"

"Don't worry about that. We will have a meeting after the press conference, but again, we will handle it," he says. "Let's get out and lie down."

We get out, and Remy dries me off before he takes me into the room. Instead of getting dressed, he has me get into bed before leaving the room. When he gets back, he is grinning.

"What?" I ask. He sets a bag in front of me, and I gasp. "Did you…"

"Order hot wings so we can sit in bed and eat? Yes," he says. "Cameron and Tris went and picked it up for us."

"I never imagined I'd be eating hot wings while naked in your bed," I say.

"As long as we don't follow this up with a blow job," he laughs, handing me napkins. We sit with our backs against the headboard and the blanket over our laps. He got me the hottest wings they sell, but he has sweet barbeque. He has never handled hot food well, but I love it.

My favorite memory of us is this right here, only I was dressed. When I needed to escape, we would sit in his bed, eat hot wings, watch movies, and I would eventually fall asleep. It has always been our thing since I was young. Even four years older, Remy and Cam have always been like best friends to me.

"Want to try one?" I ask Remy. He laughs, but doesn't say no. "They aren't that hot."

"You are part demon. It's not hot if the hellfire burns within you," he teases. I clean my hands with napkins before I move his empty food container. He laughs again when I throw the covers off him so I can climb into his lap to straddle him.

"Kiss me," I say sweetly. He gently holds my face and presses his lips against mine. As we got lost in our kiss, he groans when he can taste the spice that lingers on my tongue. When I pull away, I laugh when he is in visible pain. "Try one, Remy."

"Kissing you shouldn't be painful," he says, squeezing my hips.

"Eat the last one, and then you can fuck me," I say with a grin.

"I might actually hurt you if I fuck you while in pain." He laughs.

"That's the idea," I tell him with a sweet smile. I lean over and grab a napkin so I can pick up my last wing. He narrows his eyes, but opens his mouth to let me feed it to him. He takes the entire flat piece in his mouth, and I slowly pull it out as he cleans it down to the bone. At the same time, I lower myself on his cock, and he groans. As he chews, I toss the bone and napkin into the container and push it off to the side.

"Fuck, that's hot," he pants after swallowing the food. "Oh my God, Lori. You're trying to kill me."

"Give me the pain, Remy. I promise I can take it," I say before kissing him. He immediately moves me so I am on my belly across the bed before pulling me up to my knees. When he surges into me, he instantly finds a speed and depth that makes me scream. He is absolutely ruthless about the way he pounds into me. I get to a point where my belly is aching, and I try to pull myself away to get him to stop pushing so deep.

"No," he growls as he pulls my arms behind my back and holds them with one hand. His other tangles in my hair to pull my head back as he drives in deeper.

"It hurts," I moan.

"Good," he growls at me again. "Fucking come for me. Show me how much you love the way I fuck this tight little cunt."

My body is trembling and shaking as my orgasm rips through me, yet he still offers no reprieve. I'm trying to straighten my body in hopes that he won't be able to push as deep as he is, but he simply releases my arms to get a tight hold on my hips. I am clawing at the bed, trying to pull myself away as he rails into me. He is yanking my hips back as he drives into me, making me cry out each time he bottoms out. I don't beg him to stop or say anything; I just come over and over again.

"Fuuuck, yes. Take my come, Little Fawn. Take every fucking drop," he groans as he explodes inside of me. We are both panting and gasping for air as we lie on the bed. An unknown amount of time passes before he rolls me onto my back. My body is still trembling, and tingles still cover my skin.

"I love you, Remington," I say softly.

"I love you too, Lorelei," he says with a sweet smile before gently kissing me.

Chapter Twelve

Lorelei

Getting out of the gate this morning was a challenge because the news vans were in our way. I think that was intentional so they could get a better look at us, but the windows in the back are blacked out. It was insanely nerve-wracking to be able to see them surround the car but know that they couldn't see us.

We are at the office, but we can't get into the lot. The detective had to call for backup to help move people because none of our employees can park, nor can we. We watch as they move closer to the building, but it allows people to start parking. I have been keeping an eye on my emails this morning. I sent something out to all the floor managers and asked for an update on whether anyone was calling in or working remotely. I also expressed that we plan on having an all staff meeting today. So far, all the managers have reported that everyone is coming in.

We hang back and let our employees get in so they are not bothered before Detective Yotes comes over to us. Cam and Remy get out and come around to me and Tris gets out on my side. I have Cam on one side of me, Remy on the other. Tris is in front of us next to the detective, and we have another cop behind us. This seems excessive until we get closer to the building, and we are swarmed. Cam and Remy keep their hand on my back and walk close to me as Tris and the detective make a path. I don't think the detective wanted Tris up there, but she is doing a better job moving them. Anytime someone doesn't move, she simply shoves them out of her way and keeps walking. This girl is just as little as me, but will happily go toe to toe with a grown man.

"Ready?" Cam asks me, and I nod.

We stop in front of the door before turning to face the crowd. Remy keeps his arm around me, and Cam stays close as well. Tris is standing next to Cam, while the detective is standing off to the side to watch us.

"Good morning," Cam says just loud enough that people shut up and listen. "I am Cameron Belmont. This is Remington Saltz, my partner, and our head of marketing, Beatris Cooper, and Lorelei Belmont. Lorelei is my little sister, Remington's partner, and our COO. Yesterday afternoon, we received word that a handful of pictures and videos of Lorelei had gone viral. We took the evening to allow Lorelei to process this before we faced the media... For transparency reasons, we will be explaining the situation, but for the well-being of my sister's mental health, Mr. Saltz and I will be the ones answering," Cam says. "It was known to our family that Lorelei worked at Northern Lights Entertainment's club, The Treasure chest, while in college. Rob Lasson was her manager and the owner of this club. Last night, he was arrested on fifteen counts of human trafficking for the events that took place in the club. No other arrests have been made. It is still an active investigation, and Lorelei is working with the police on this matter, as these things do not wrap up overnight. Now, to be specific, Lorelie worked at the club as a dancer but was a victim of trafficking. Rob Lasson has openly admitted to forcing the girls into the backrooms so that clients could pay to use them how they saw fit in. Lorelei is working through her trauma, and we are supporting her every step of the way.

"There have been statements made that she was using solicitation as a way to blackmail executives into doing business dealings with Saltz-Belmont Technologies, and I assure you that is wildly inaccurate. It is slanderous not only to her character, but to the character of our business as well. The individual making these claims is a client of ours, but we are under contract. We have every intention of honoring this contract, but as her brother and Remington's partner, we will be conducting business in a way that protects her.

"Lorelei is a brilliant woman who is wonderful at her job. It is disgusting that anyone would think it's okay to release photos and videos of her like that. It is sexist on many levels that she is being shamed and questioned, but the other individual is not. With Rob Lasson in custody, we are urging everyone to respect Lorelei's wishes and respect her privacy moving forward. Remington and I will continue to support her, and none of this has any bearing on how we conduct business.

"If Lorelei chooses to make a statement, it will be at a later date," Remington says simply before we turn to go into the building. Insults are hurled at me like weapons from a group of protesters off to one side, and Cam grabs Tris and pulls her into the building before she can say anything.

"Fucking ridiculous," Tris grumbles.

"We have a last-minute meeting with our clients and board members," Cam says to Detective Yotes.

"I would love to join, if you'll have me," he says coolly.

"That's not a problem," Remy says. I, on the other hand, get pissed. When we step into the elevator, I turn and snap at him.

"Are you investigating me? What reason do you have to attend this meeting?" I ask. He looks at me for a second and doesn't say anything, so I roll my eyes. "Whatever."

"Why are you acting so defensively?" he asks.

"You are really fucking annoying, you know that?" I ask, glaring at him.

"You and my ex-wife would get along wonderfully," he says with a smirk. "Bluntly?"

"Yes," I say with a frown.

"I think you, those other girls, and Rob are all full of shit," he says. "I think all of you were willing, and Rob is taking the fall so that you girls don't get in trouble."

I say nothing because he is right. I am a shitty liar, and he sees right through me. He sighs and pulls the emergency stop before turning to me. "Detective," Cam says with a warning in his tone.

"Relax, big brother," Detective Yotes says, making Tris chuckle. "Lorelei, I can help you, but I need you to tell me the truth. The full truth. I have no interest in throwing a bunch of people in jail when no one is getting hurt. My job is to catch and shut down trafficking rings. If that isn't the case here, I need to know."

I shake my head and back myself into the corner. I slide down the wall to sit and Tris glares at Cam and Remy until they back up. The detective comes over and sits beside me. "I can't," I whimper.

"What can I do to earn your trust?" he asks.

"Go away," I sniff, and he laughs.

"Well, I can't do that. I'd love to explain more, but I need for you to be truthful," he says. "How about this... How about I tell you what Rob told me when I told him of my suspicions that he was lying to help you girls?"

"Okay..."

"He said he was guilty, and I couldn't prove otherwise," he tells me. "Now... I have been doing this a long time, and I have talked to many individuals guilty of running girls... He is the kindest and most considerate trafficker I have ever met. Weird, huh?"

"Mhmm..."

"When I asked what kind of punishments he'd give for running, not paying their cut, unsatisfied clients, and so on, he shut down. He couldn't say one thing he had done to you all... I asked the girls the same thing, and nothing. No one is going into detail," he tells me. "Lorelei... I know the truth, and honestly, I don't need you to confirm it. I like for you to admit it because there are things I need to explain, but I can't if you are sticking with the story that Rob made you."

"I'm not going to jail," I say.

"You won't go to jail. You won't be getting charged. My boss has expressed that they knew about this club and that it wasn't trafficking, so no one has tried shutting it down."

"What?" I ask.

"Lorelei... We've had undercover agents in that club numerous times and you know what is always found?"

"What?" I ask.

"The girls are happy, taken care of, no one is on drugs, the girls have personal vehicles, clients pay the girls, not Rob... We have not found one indication that girls are being forced in there," he says. "Also... an agent has been with you, Lorelei."

"Oh hell," I sigh. "It was the weird guy that just talked, wasn't it?" I ask with a sigh.

"Yes. His name is Heath," he chuckles. "We have never had an owner who ran the girls also run background checks on the clients... But Rob did. His rules were strict, too."

"Not strict enough," I grumble.

"What do you mean?" he asks. I sigh heavily and back my head back against the wall before looking up at Cam and Remy.

"Meh. Worst-case, we will bail you out and run," Tris says. "Hypothetically..."

"Fine," I sigh. "Rob never made anyone do anything. He let us make our own choices. He took care of us and made sure we were safe. I was there because I was trying to rewrite my trauma from being violently raped in high school..."

"But you've gotten hurt there before?" he asks. I look at Remy and just shake my head. "Understand that I already know all the answers to the questions I'm asking you."

"Then why the fuck are you asking?" I snap.

"Because it's your story, Lorelei," he says. "Look... The three men last seen at that club that someone took a bat to had cameras in their home planted by me and my boss."

"Then you should know who did it then. Why are you here?" I ask.

"Because Remington was smart enough to wear a mask, Lorelei," he says.

"Then what the fuck do you want from me?" I yell at him before standing up and hitting the emergency stop. I scan my badge so it will take us to the top floor instead so I can go to my office. When the doors open, I storm out ahead of everyone and go to my office. I try to slam my door shut, but the detective puts his foot in the way to stop it. "Go away."

"I'm trying to be gentle here, because I know you have been through a lot. You aren't responding to that, so I am going to be blunt," he says. "Those two men were wanted in connection to the disappearance of Nadia Jenkins."

"What?" I ask. "Dia... She..."

"Was a dancer at the club. I know. We sent undercover agent in over and over again because we thought for sure Rob was guilty, but it never panned out," he says. "George Hamilton was the last client she saw before she went missing. Two other men joined him. After she went home that night, she was never seen alive. Her body was recovered last week, she had been held for six months before eventually dying."

"Wait," Remy says. "Six months?"

"Oh.... Fuck," I say. "Oh, no..."

"The two men he brought in with him are named Jose Miranda and Julio Martinez. They are connected to a ring that traffics girls, and George... Well, he is thought to run everything. He picks the girls, and those two men carry out his orders," he continues.

"I kept seeing someone in my apartment building over the last six months. I never saw their face, but if I was in the elevator after dark, he was there," I say. "George... He has been coming to see me since I started there."

"But he never could get close enough," Remy says.

"Exactly," Detective Yotes says. "Rob was moved to a different location for his safety. Many of the girls also were moved as a precaution, but you were their target. Those men who got their brains beat in had your picture, a copy of the key to your apartment, and your daily schedule. They saw you on that Friday night, yes?"

"Yeah," I sigh.

"Rob said they expressed to you that they'd come back the next day," he says. "If it weren't for Remington... doing what Remington does... They would have taken you. They tried many times, I think, because there were some text exchanges on their phones talking about Remington always being around and getting in the way."

"So, if they are dead…"

"It does not mean you are safe," he says. "It just means that I now have no idea who is running the ring or who will come after you."

"Fuck," Cam says. "Her face is all over the goddamn media."

"Yeah. Your client is either guilty of being involved or just a massive asshole," the detective says.

"Detective Yotes…"

"Just Ross," he says.

"Ross, Matthew came to see me a lot," I say.

"For how long?" he asks.

"Years," I say. "Twice a month on Saturdays."

"So, not the same nights as George?"

"No," I say. "What the fuck do I do? I won't endanger them. My family didn't do anything, they didn't do anything and I won't be the reason they get hurt. I don't even know what I'm supposed to do. I've never…"

"Stop. Slow down and breathe," Ross says.

"Will you people stop telling me to fucking breathe?!" I yell at him as tears roll down my face. Remy comes around my desk and hugs me. I instantly fall apart and he scoops me up to sit in my chair with me. "I'm so scared."

"I know, baby. I've got you," he murmurs into my hair as he holds me tightly.

"What are we supposed to do to keep her safe?" Cam asks.

"First, when she is ready, you go into that meeting. You say the exact same thing you told the press, and you take no shit," Ross says. "You fake it if you have to, but show that none of this is affecting you all. Continue business as usual, but you *never* leave her alone. I will be around as much as I possibly can."

"They are supposed to go across the country for a meeting soon. Can they still do to that?" Cam asks.

"Yes," he says. "Company jet?"

"Yeah," Remy says.

"I'm sorry," I say as I sit up and wipe my face.

"Not a problem," Ross says.

"Ready to do this?" Remy asks me.

"Yeah," I sigh.

"I think she should speak, especially if Matthew will be there," Ross says. "And really lay it on thick with them."

"I agree," Cam says. "You okay with that?"

"Yeah," I say. I stand and we all walk out. This time, we take the stairs down one floor and go to the conference room that we are using today. When we walk in, everyone stops talking and stares at me.

"Good morning, everyone," I say. A few murmur a response, but everyone is quiet for the most part. I don't sit because I will explode. Cam and Remy stay standing with me, but Tris and the detective stand off to the side. "I'm going to get right into it, I guess... I know you all are here because of the video. I am going to be more blunt with you all than we were with the media because you deserve an explanation; I owe them nothing. Tris, can you take notes of their questions along the way so I can make sure I answer them?"

"I sure can," she smiles.

"Okay. I worked in that club while in college," I say. "I was always a dancer, but it was a form of coping after being having been raped in high school. I was young and dumb, so I didn't think that I would ever get wrapped up in something bad. It was just dancing after all... Well, that quickly escalated into me being forced to do things I never wanted to do. I will spare you the details, but I knew the consequences would be severe if I didn't do as I was told. I was too ashamed to tell my family for a while, so I just did what I was told and kept the peace as best I could... I was able to maintain my normal life because I guess I had proven that I would be obedient. I was, for a while. I eventually worked up the courage to tell Cameron and Remington. They knew I still worked there and were patient with me as I processed the horrific trauma I endured as a teenager. When I finally spoke up about what I was being made to do, they helped me escape... For transparency, it was only recently that I managed to get away. Yesterday, an individual here decided that getting a hold of pictures and videos to show only a fraction of the situation would be worthy of trying to blackmail us into paying ten million dollars to not have it released. We ultimately refused, and they released it... This led to the arrest of Rob Lasson, my boss at the club and the one making us do things with clients who paid well... This individual came to the club, knowing exactly who I was. It appears they had planned to try blackmailing me one day.

"I realize this doesn't paint me in a good light to some, but I have never, and would never involve, this company in that. I kept them very far apart, and I have never blackmailed anyone into anything. Simply put, this person did help all of those girls escape by exposing what was going on, but also failed to accomplish anything. They shared pictures and videos of an encounter that I was forced into... I do not think the clients knew we were forced, but we were, nonetheless.

"This individual will not be named, and we will not be seeking to terminate the contract. We do not expect any backlash from this, so business will not be affected... Does anyone have any questions?"

"I do," Leann Porter, a board member, asks. "Will the board members know the name of the client?"

"Yes," Cam says.

"Why not just say it now, then?" she asks.

"I have no problem saying his name, but unlike him, I have no desire to tear someone down. Bluntly, I know he is full of shit, but if he felt he had no other choice, who am I to correct him?"

"By a show of hands," Remy says. "Who thinks the name should be released to allow them a chance to defend themselves?"

They all raise their hand, and Matthew looks nervous. "Matthew Hernandez," I say.

"Ten million, dude?" Alan Jacobs asks. Matthew says nothing as he stares at me.

"Matthew, you are free to speak. This is not one sided," I say.

"I didn't know you were being forced," he says after a long pause. "If I had known, I would have come to Cameron and Remington."

"Oh?" Tris laughs. "You would have gone to her highly protective older brother and even more protective boyfriend and told them what? You went into the club to fuck her, but you think she might be being forced into it?"

"Well… No… When you put it that way," he says, making me smile.

"Why did you try to get them to pay you?" Leann asks.

"Truthfully… Because we are suffering," he says. "We are one bad month away from filing for bankruptcy."

"I'll make you a deal," Cam says. "If the board objects, we can talk about it, but we will buy 75% percent of your stocks and let you continue to run it."

"We need an in-depth audit first," Remington adds. "Get us that by the end of the week, and so long as the decline isn't from theft, we can fix the situation and let you run it."

"Let me run the audit and I'll decide by the time I get done," he says. "I… shit… I need to talk to my wife first…"

"Oh shit," Tris laughs.

"Okay," Cam chuckles.

"Does anyone have any questions?" Remy asks.

"We would like to vote on removing Lorelei as COO," Leann says.

Yeah, I knew that was coming, but I don't expect Cameron's response. "Okay. Vote," he says.

"All in favor?" Remington asks casually. I am *shocked* when all ten board members raise their hand.

"Well, fuck you guys too," I mutter to myself.

"Lorelei," Cameron says with a smirk. "The board has voted to remove you as COO and we will be taking their suggestion."

"Okay," I say, narrowing my eyes at him.

"Tris?" he says.

"Yes." she smiles.

"We are formally offering you the position of COO. Do you accept?"

"I do," she says.

"Wonderful," Remington says, taking a folder from her. "Lorelei?"

"Yes?" I ask, narrowing my eyes at him.

"Sign, please," he says, handing me a pen. I take it and step closer to see that it is paperwork to make me a third owner.

"Go on," Cam says, nudging me. I shake my head at him but turn and sign the paper. He and Remy sign before handing it to Tris to sign.

"Lorelei is officially a third owner of Saltz-Belmont. We will be sure to get her information changed for everyone," Remington says.

"I'm confused, but okay," I say.

"They had been planning on doing this for a few months," Leann says with a smile. "We support you entirely."

"I appreciate that," I say with a smile. Ross smiles at me and it seems as though he might have known too. "Well, unless anyone has any questions, you all are free to go."

"Matthew, hang back for me," Ross says.

Once everyone is gone, Matthew looks *terrified*. "Who are you?" he asks.

"I am Detective Ross Yotes. I work with organized crime and the human trafficking division," he says.

"I swear to God, I didn't know," Matthew says. "I didn't."

"Did anyone there ever stick out to you?"

"Like other clients?" he asks. "Not really. I never interacted with anyone but Lorelei and one other girl."

"If you think of *anything*, it would be in your best interest to tell me," Ross says. "Understand?"

"Yes," Matthew says with a rapid nod. He gets up and rushes out, and I shake my head.

"It's crazy," I say. "He was so confident yesterday."

"Mhmm. It happens like that," Ross chuckles.

"Aw. How are we going to get lunch today with the media?" I ask.

"I'll run out and get it," Tris says. "I can go by that sushi place."

"Oh, I love sushi," I smile.

"You'll eat anything that doesn't eat you first," Tris says, making Cam and Remy chuckle.

"So how about this?" Cam says. "We can prep for the all-staff meeting and lead that. Tris, you can go grab lunch, since that might take a little more time than usual to pick up."

"Works for me," I say. "Ross. Lunch?"

"I'm okay," he smiles.

"That's not what I asked you," I say. "Offended by raw meat?"

"It's…"

"Ross. Answer the damn question," I scold.

"I'll eat anything," he says with a smirk playing at his lips.

"Put it on my card, Tris," Cam says.

"Cam," I sigh.

"Suck it up," he says. "My card, Tris."

"Okay," she laughs. "Love you, guys. I'm going to go do that."

"Love you too," Cam says as he kisses her. Remy hugs her before I walk around to do the same.

"Thank you for always supporting me," I say as I hug her tightly. "I love you so much, Tris."

"I love you, Lori. Best bitches forever," she says with a bright smile. "Bye, Ross."

"Bye, Tris," Ross smiles.

Chapter Thirteen

Beatris

THE DAY FEELS WEIRD, despite the obvious. I am happy to be getting out of that office and away from the chaos. I fucking hate that they are hounding Lorelei like this. She doesn't deserve any of it. So what if she wanted to fuck for some extra cash? I sure as hell would have. Cam will never admit this to her, but he has seen her dance before and had suspected she was doing it, anyway. He said the times he went there to check on her, she always ended up in one of the back rooms, so I think it was always assumed that she was doing more.

I walk out of the back entrance to the building and step into the alleyway. I hate going this way, but it keeps me away from the media circus. Despite the fact that they're up our ass, it's a beautiful day. Sometimes it's hard to look up at the sky and enjoy the sunshine when clouds loom overhead. I hope that Lorelei notices the sun eventually. She's a strong girl, so I have no doubt that she will find a way to navigate all of this, even if it is piling on little-by-little overtime.

I make it to the sushi restaurant and pick up our order before walking back toward the office. It's early still, but I have to go through the main entrance to get back in. I cut down the alleyway to get to the front of the building. I get about halfway down when a crowd of people moves in front of the entrance.

"Are you fucking kidding?" I deadpan. I'll never get through all of those people. I turn to go back the way I came, and panic washes over me. There is a black van blocking the exit and a man in a ski mask walking toward me. Two others come around the van, and I freeze.

No matter how many times I scream at my body to just turn and fucking run, I don't. I stand there with tears rolling down my cheeks, fully understanding what's going on. When they get within ten feet, I finally bolt. I don't get far before one of them grabs me by the hair and yanks me back. My mouth is covered by a calloused hand before I can scream, and I am swiftly picked up and carried toward the van. I thrash and scream against the hand. Trying to get away. Trying to survive. Why didn't I run? Why did I just fucking stand there? I could be inside right now instead of being hauled into a van.

The moment the van door shuts, a bag is pulled over my head and my arms are tied behind my back.

"Stop!" I scream, then my pants are yanked off my legs. "Stop! Please stop."

A man places his hands on my shoulder blades as I am pinned face down in this van and grunts as he shoves himself deep into my ass. A shrill scream rips from my throat as he starts fucking me hard and deep, desperately searching for release. "Fuck, this bitch is tight," he groans. "Stupid fucking whore. Are you crying?"

"Stop," I whimper. "Please."

"Yeah," a man says. "Yep. We got her... Dumb bitch left the office without her brother or boyfriend... Yeah... see ya."

Fuck, they think I'm Lorelei. What the fuck am I supposed to do now? If I tell them I'm not, they will just go after her. I'd rather die than let her get hurt like this. The moment they grabbed me, I knew I was dead. There is no coming back from this.

The man fucking my ass moans in my ear as he rails into me. My body has gone limp, and I am just laying here. Memories of my life with Cameron, Lorelei, and Remington play through my mind, and I find solace in knowing I am saving Lorelei from this cruelty. Cameron is going to be devastated, but he has Lori and Remy to help him get through my loss. I wonder how quickly they'll find my body. Will they ever? They have so much going on today; it will take them a while to notice I'm gone. They'll blame themselves for letting me leave alone, but I knew better than to walk through the alleyway. I never should have gone that way, but my laziness contributed to that deadly mistake.

When the man comes, another replaces him, and he takes me harder and deeper. I whimper every time he slams deep, but thankfully, he doesn't last as long as the other man. He comes and I am left on the floor of the van with an ass full of come and a bag over my head. The zip ties are so tight that I can't feel my fingers, but I don't care. I feel like I'm already dead, but I am waiting for my heart to get the memo and stop beating.

Several minutes pass before the van comes to a stop and I am dragged out. Someone picks me up, tossing me over their shoulder, and I'm carried off somewhere. "Put her on the bed," a familiar voice says.

I am dropped on a mattress, and I am restrained so that my arms and legs are tied to each corner of the bed. The rest of my clothing is cut off, but the bag stays in place. I wonder how mad they will be when they realize they grabbed the wrong woman?

"Anyone seen you?" The familiar voice asks.

"Nope. She cut through the alleyway, and we grabbed her," a man says.

"Good job, boys," the familiar voice says closer to me. He grabs hold of the bag and when he yanks it off, I am instantly terrified for Lorelei. She will never expect this level of betrayal. "Are you fucking kidding me? Are you fucking stupid?"

"What?" a man asks.

"That's not Lorelei, you fucking moron," he screams. Three shots go off, one right after another, and I am stunned. I say nothing. I do nothing. I lay here wide-eyed and willing to die to keep Lorelei safe from this evil. How will she recover from this when she finds out she was betrayed by someone she cared about?

"Well, what the fuck am I going to do with you?" He asks as he turns to me. "You've seen my face now."

"Why would you do this to her?" I ask with a small voice. "She cares about you."

"She is a dumb whore who cares about those who kiss her ass," he snaps. "Either you call her and find a way to get her here alone, or you're dead."

"Get creative when you kill me," I say coldly.

He huffs out his laughter as he takes his belt off. He tosses it on my belly as he gets naked. This man is huge all around, and I am fucking terrified of how much pain I'm about to be in. I know my death won't be fast or painless. He is going to torture me and love every goddamn second of it.

I may not be able to save myself, but I can die knowing that Lorelei is safe right now. They will have each other to lean on, and my death will help the police figure out who this monster is. I refuse to beg because I know death is inevitable. I will endure this pain because the longer he takes with me, the less time he has to get to Lorelei.

He grabs the belt, and I squeeze my eyes shut. Seconds later, he swings it down, and the pain slices through me as I am hit with the belt. I am instantly brought to sobs as he wails on me, letting out his frustration that I am not who he wanted me to be. My screams are quickly becoming ragged and hoarse, but I never mutter a word. I won't beg. I won't say anything. I will not give him the satisfaction of feeling as though he broke me.

By the time he stops hitting me, my voice is gone, and my screams are no louder than a whisper. My entire body is on fire, and he is breathing heavily. He climbs on top of me and rams himself into my pussy. The friction makes me groan as more pain shoots through my belly. He chuckles and slams in again, forcing another grunt out of me. I still haven't opened my eyes, and I won't.

"Look at me, whore," he screams. When I don't, he slaps me. "Stupid fucking bitch."

He starts fucking me hard and fast, making fresh tears fall. I can smell the metallic scent permeating the air around us. I also know that I'm bleeding based on how the friction disappears from his thrusts. Another scream racks from my throat when he leans in and bites down on the top of my shoulder. I can feel his teeth puncture my flesh, and my entire body reacts by violently shaking, and my breathing is coming in short bursts from the intense pain radiating from my shoulder. I'm certain he just took an entire chunk out of my shoulder. Warmth is spreading around my back and neck, confirming that I'm bleeding.

"You'll regret being such a loyal friend, sweet Beatris," he says softly in my ear. "All you had to do was bring her to me."

"Lorelei will be the death of you," I choke out, content with my final words.

"And I will be the death of you," he laughs, his manic voice echoing in my brain long after he stops.

Minutes pass, and he seems to be gone. I know he will be back, so every noise makes me jump. I am annoyed that he is dragging this out and terrified that he can somehow make this more painful. When he spreads me open more and something is clamped onto my clit, it is nearly enough to break me. He pulls out until I whimper in pain and wait for him to do it. I don't know how I know, but it is on par with his torture so far.

When the blade slices into me, I am nearly convulsing as a sudden and loud scream rips its way out of me. The pain is unlike anything I have ever felt and even if I wanted to beg for death, I cannot form anything but desperate screams. I start violently gagging and retching when he forces my flesh down my throat. His hand is covered in my blood as he makes me swallow my own clit.

I must be going into shock because I hardly feel it when he immediately slams the knife into my pussy, shoving as deep into my abdomen as he can. There is someone else here, but my brain is rejecting the voice I am hearing. There is no way.

I am still screaming as he starts fucking me with the blade, making blood nearly gush out of me. The only thing I can feel is the warmth of my blood and the chilly air surrounding me. My face feels cold, and I am quickly weakening.

He cuts my limbs free before tossing the knife aside. When he climbs back on the bed, he grabs the backs of my knees and pushes my knees to my chest. He resumes fucking me as hard and fast as he can, but this time he wants to see if he can finish before I die. I have still yet to open my eyes because I refuse to let him be the last thing I see.

I want to be sad, but I'm not. I know I will be grieved, and it will nearly destroy all of them, but they will survive. My death will be what drives them to solve this and save not just Lorelei but every other woman that would have otherwise been subjected to what I have been. My death will not be in vain.

As I feel myself starting to slip away, it's them that I picture. Cameron, Lorelei, and Remington smiling brightly at me, and I can feel their love drawing me in, telling me it's okay to give up. It's okay to move on without them. I am passing without regret or worries, and that is the best thing I could have ever asked for. A warm light takes over my mind, and I become weightless. Even from far away, I can feel their presence as the world fades.

Chapter Fourteen
Detective Ross Yotes

It never gets easier. No matter how many times I come to a crime scene, the sight of their body still cuts through my soul, taking pieces of it to disappear with the souls of the dead.

"Time of death?" I ask.

"No more than an hour," the medical examiner tells me.

"Damn," my boss, Andrea Hall, says as she steps beside me. "Have they noticed that she's gone?"

"No," I sigh. "They started prep for the all-staff meeting, and they are in that right now. They knew she left to get lunch, but they won't really be looking for her until after the meeting."

"How did you know she was missing?" Andrea asks.

"I was working on notes while they were prepping and realized she was still gone. I messaged Carlson and asked him to call the sushi place, and they said she had left the restaurant already. When they went into the meeting, I left Carlson there and went to look around. Her bag and the food were in the alleyway beside the office," I explain. "They don't even know that Beatris is missing, and now I have to tell them she's dead."

"Want me to do it?" she asks.

"No, but I'd like for you to be there," I say. "I think they will gravitate toward one another, but I'd just like for them to see you so they know we are working to find who did this."

"Remington is the one who worries me," she says.

"They level each other out, and I'll make sure Cameron and Lorelei's parents are there as well. It's Lorelei that I'm worried about," I tell her. "I'm afraid she will do something reckless to try and prevent someone else from getting hurt."

"Those girls look alike, so they probably just thought she was Lorelei, but that won't make her feel any better," Andrea says. "Miranda?"

"Yes, ma'am?" The medical examiner asks as she continues to examine Beatris' body.

"If they ask to view her, do not explain her injuries. Do not let them see any wounds. I don't care if they want to sign a release or not. They will not know the details of the murder unless it goes to trial," Andrea says.

"I am going to heavily suggest they do not see her," I say.

"Get a picture of just her face, and we can show that if they want to see her," Andrea says. "We also need to officially offer witness protection."

"They won't take it," I say.

"I know, but they need to know we are trying to protect them. I want you with them at all times. If you can't be with them, I will be. We will rotate out, so they are never alone."

"Okay," I sigh and tap on my phone to capture a picture of Beatris' face. I crop the image to make sure the massive wound on her shoulder isn't visible.

"If you had to guess a cause of death?" Andrea asks Miranda.

"Uh... well... Her clitoris was cut off, and the perineum has been completely cut into her rectum. I'm going to say someone raped her with a very large knife," she says carefully. "The amount of blood loss tells me that the wounds extend up into the abdomen. She has semen on top of this blood, so I'm going to say that he probably raped her after raping her with the knife. So... massive blood loss."

"Goddamn it," I snap. "What the fuck do I even tell them, Andrea?"

"Ross, you've done this before, man. Be blunt but not crude. Leave no room for doubt and be empathetic," Andrea says.

"I hate this fucking job sometimes," I grumble.

Chapter Fifteen

Lorelei

"Does anyone have any more questions?" I ask. Please, God, no more questions.

"Okay. You all are dismissed," Cam says with a sigh. We have all been checking our phones nonstop to see where Tris is. She's been gone forever and we've been stuck in this damn meeting. I love our employees, but they ask so many questions.

"Nothing?" I ask Cam when he looks at his phone.

"No," he frowns. I turn and look around to find Ross standing with a woman.

"Hey," I say as I walk up to him. "We have been trying for a while now to get ahold of Tris, but she's not answering. Have you seen her?"

"Why don't we go back to yours and Remington's house to talk?" he says.

"No," I snap.

"What's wrong?" Remy asks.

"I asked where Tris is, and he wants us to go home," I say as fear bubbles in my chest.

"Lorelei," he starts to say, but I shake my head.

"No. I want to know where Tris is," I say as tears roll down my cheeks. I have an awful feeling based on the sad look in his eyes.

"Lorelei, I need you to listen," he says as he gently holds my shoulders so I won't turn away. "You do not want to do this in front of your employees. Okay? Home is best."

"Oh no," Remy says. Tears start to choke me out as I realize what he is telling me. I refuse to believe it, though. There's no way. We just saw her in the conference room three hours ago.

"You parents are meeting us there. Please go straight home, okay?" Ross says to me.

"What's going on?" Cam says.

"Let's go home," I say to Cam.

"But what about..." Cam starts to ask.

"Cameron, please," I whimper. "Let's meet Mom and Dad at the house." The realization sweeps over him and watching my brother's heart shatter in front of me is almost too much to bear.

"Ross, you drive them. I'll follow with your car," the woman says softly. He nods and waves us along.

We are all almost zombie-like as we go outside to the car. I notice the alleyway is blocked off by crime scene tape. I look at Ross, and he just sighs.

I sit between Cam and Remy in the back as Ross drives us to the house. They have a tight grip on my hands, knowing that is what is holding me together right now. We know what has happened, but no one is willing to say it aloud.

When the gate shuts behind us, we drive up and park beside Mom and Dad. The second we are out, I run into the house, hoping to find Tris waiting on us. Instead, I find my parents, who look like they have both been sobbing.

"Oh, honey," Mom says tearfully.

"They don't know," Ross says. "Guys, come sit with me."

"No," I say. "No. I'm not sitting. Where is Tris? Where is she?"

"Lorelei, please come sit with me," Ross says gently.

"No," I yell at him as fresh tears flood my face.

"Come on, baby. Sit with us," Remy says softly, pulling me toward the couch. I sit in the center with Cam on one side and Remy on the other. Mom and Dad are standing together, and the woman is standing by the door.

"Who is she?" I ask, trying to distract myself from the obvious.

"Andrea Hall. She is my boss," Ross says. "Lorelei..."

"Please don't say it," I say tearfully.

"Lorelei, Beatris is dead," he says bluntly.

The sob that comes out of me is filled with pain and sadness. I try to get up, but both Cam and Remy grab me in a tight hug as I completely fall apart. I reach a point where I can't breathe, so Cameron pulls me into his lap and rocks me.

"It's my fault," I choke out. I say it over and over again, guilt slowly eating away at me.

"No, Lori. No. It's not your fault," Cam says as he holds my chin so I can't look away from him. "It's not your fault. I promise. Okay? This isn't on you."

"She's dead," I whimper. "My best friend is dead."

"Sit up here so we can find out more," he encourages. He helps me sit up, and Ross has tears in his eyes.

"What happened?" I ask, wiping my face.

"She was taken on her way back from getting food," he says. "She used the back alleyway, and we think she was cornered there... She was taken to an abandoned house about twenty minutes down the road. An elderly lady living a little bit down the road called in a report for screams. Police called me when they got into the house."

"How?" Cam asks.

"Blood loss," he says vaguely.

"Did she suffer?" I ask.

"Yes," he says. "It was fast in the sense that she died before you had even officially started the meeting."

"Was it meant to be me? We look alike," I say.

"I believe so. Her injuries are extremely similar to that of other women we've seen killed by this group," he says.

"What were her injuries?" Remy asks, and Ross sighs.

"Ross," I snap. He looks at his boss, and she shrugs.

"Lorelei, I'm not sure if you want to imagine her this way," he says softly.

"It was meant to be me," I say as tears well up. "I want to know what would have happened to me."

"She was tortured," he says after a moment of silence. "She had marks that tell me she was likely whipped with something from her neck to her shins. She was violently assaulted and mutilated."

"How did she die of blood loss then?" Cam asks.

"She was assaulted with a knife," Andrea says when Ross doesn't. "The autopsy will confirm, but it caused significant damage from the onset, based on what we've seen."

"Can we see her?" I ask quietly.

"Hun, I don't really think that's a good idea," Ross says. "I have a picture of just her face that I can show you, but I think it would be best if you didn't see her like this."

"Okay," I whimper.

I cover my mouth to keep the sobs from escaping when he turns his phone around for us to see. Her eyes are closed but her skin is a grayish color. It's subtle, but you can tell that she is gone. She looks to be at peace, despite what her body endured. I have no doubts that she died just as stubborn as she lived. She was fiercely protective of me. I think she fought with everything she had, even if only mentally.

"I am so sorry," Ross says softly. "I think this is the point where we need to get you all in witness protection."

"No," I sniff.

"Lorelei, this proves that they are after you," he says.

"I don't care. I'm not running," I say. "We have a company to run."

"Cameron? Remington?" Ross asks.

"It's up to her," Cam says, rubbing my back.

"Cameron will come stay here with us," Remington says. "She will never be alone."

"Mom? Dad?" I ask.

"We are going to go to the hunting cabin," Dad says softly.

"Okay," I say. "I'm supposed to be her executor, so I guess I'll have to sign for her to go to a funeral home?"

"Yes," Ross says. "I'll get the medical examiner to call you when she can be released."

"Okay," I say simply.

"Lorelei," Ross says.

"What, Ross?" I ask.

"You can't be reckless," he says. "I know you are going to try and protect everyone, but you can't do that here. Okay?"

"I won't let anyone else get hurt," I say.

"If you go and get yourself killed, she will have died for nothing," Mom speaks up. "We all know that girl was likely given a chance to give you up and she would have been stubborn to the very end."

"Yeah," I whisper. "I won't survive if I lose anyone else… if I hadn't worked there…"

"Stop," Remy says, turning my face to meet his. "What would she tell you right now?"

"That it's okay to be selfish and protect myself," I say tearfully.

"Right, so let us protect you like we know she did," he says. "Cam and I will be right here with you every step of the way, and I swear to God, you will survive this. You will go on to live a happy life in her memory."

"She can't be gone," I say tearfully.

"She's gone, baby," he says softly. "I want to fix it, but I can't. All we can do is move forward and honor her the best we can."

"Andrea and I will rotate being with you all," Ross says. "I'll be here tonight, so if you need anything at all, I will be outside with another cop. Andrea will be here in the morning."

"Okay," I say. "I don't know what to do from here."

"Right now, just be with your family," Ross says. "We will keep you updated on the investigation the best we can. Let us know if anyone reaches out or you see anything out of the ordinary. Otherwise, just... live your life."

"She was just made COO," I say. "I feel stupid for being worried about that."

"We can have Sam take over marketing," Cam sighs. "We will dissolve the COO position, and we all take over those duties."

"Sam will do well. Tris did great training him," Remy says.

"Tomorrow I'd like to tell the employees," I say before looking at Ross. "Can I make a statement to the press on this?"

"Andrea?" Ross asks.

"That would be a good idea," she says. "We can let you announce her death; it just needs to be first thing tomorrow if you can manage.

"Okay," I say.

"I'm going to walk Andrea out," Ross says. "If you need anything, and I mean it, just come down and sit with me."

I stand when Mom and Dad do, and they both hug me. "I'm so sorry, baby," Mom sniffles.

"We love you so, so much," Dad adds.

"I love y'all too," I say before turning to Ross. I abruptly hug him, and it takes him a second to hug me back. "Thank you, Ross."

"I'm so sorry about Tris," he says softly.

"Just find who did this to her," I say as I pull back and wipe my face. "I feel... like I'm not taking this hard enough."

"Grief looks different for everyone," he says. "Just remember, you are surrounded by people that love and support you."

"Yeah," I sigh. Mom and Dad hug Cam and Remy before pulling back and wiping their tears away.

"Do we have to wait to do the funeral?" I ask. "I don't want to hold Mom and Dad back from being able to get to the cabin."

"No, you just obviously cannot do a burial," he says.

"She wanted to be cremated anyway, so I'll just do a memorial," I say.

"You don't have to plan it alone," Cam says.

"I know. I just need to focus on something. This and work will do. I will process over time," I say.

"Let me know when you are planning the funeral, and I will make sure we have plenty of officers available so that everyone is safe," Andrea says, and I nod.

"I'm going to go upstairs," I say to Remy before I turn and go to the stairs.

"Cam, go with her, please," Remy says. I ignore that and just go to the bedroom. I take my shoes off before walking into the bathroom and turning the shower on.

"I'd suggest you go away, unless you want to see me naked," I say to Cam as I pull my shirt off and toss it in the hamper.

"I don't trust that you aren't about to hurt yourself," he says as he watches me from the doorway. I stare at him with a blank expression as I unbutton my pants and push them past my hips so that they pool at my feet. I step out and toss them into the hamper before checking the water. I am seeing just how far I can push him before he gets uncomfortable and leaves, but he doesn't budge. I unhook my bra, and I turn slightly so I can toss it on the counter. When I turn back, he is scanning my body.

Interesting.

I pull my panties down and let them drop, dragging his eyes down my body again. When I toss them into the hamper, Remy walks in. "If you think you'll make him uncomfortable, you are going to lose," he says as he checks the temperature of the water. He adjusts it so that it is cooler, and I frown at him. "Cam, you have to watch when she takes a shower because she tries to burn her fucking skin off in the process. The water here gets hot as fuck, so if I am not around, check and make sure she isn't trying to hurt herself."

"Noted," Cam says simply, still looking at me.

"Do you need help?" Remy asks me.

"I want you two to leave me alone," I say.

"Not a chance in hell," Cam says.

"If you need help, I will get in with you. If you don't, we will stay out here," Remy says. "Either way, I will kick your ass if you try to make that hotter."

"I don't know," I admit.

"We will get in with you," Remy says.

"We?" I ask, raising an eyebrow.

"Yeah, we. You're butt ass naked in front of Cameron right now. I think you can handle seeing his dick," he says. I shrug and step into the shower as they start to undress.

These two men are my best friends. Tris was my best friend, too. The four of us have been extremely close, especially in the last eight years. Growing up, Cam and Remy were always there. They are still here now, but it's different now that we are older. Things have changed over time, and we have grown more comfortable with each other. This isn't the first time I have caught Cam looking at my body, and I would be a damn liar if I said I didn't look at him either. I feel like I should be ashamed of looking at him the same way I do Remy, but I don't.

Cam and Remy step into the shower with me and turn on the other shower heads so the water is raining down on all of us. I have my head tipped back so that it hits my neck and chest, and I try to relax. Is that what you are supposed to do in these moments? One of the guys starts washing my hair, and I groan when his nails drag across my scalp.

"I'm your brother, Lori. You can't be making those noises when I touch you," Cam teases.

"Don't make it feel so good then," I mutter.

"Should I feel jealous?" Remy laughs.

"You are the one who let another naked man in the shower with me," I say. "I'm sad. What do I care?"

"Look at me," Remy says. I pull my head up to look at him and Cam continues to wash my hair. "We are going to be okay, Lori."

"Yeah, but she's not," I say. "She's dead and we are in the shower making jokes."

"Baby, we can't do anything about it. No matter what we do, it's not going to bring her back," he says. "Tris would be the first one to start cracking jokes, and you know that. She would want you to grieve her however is easiest and safest. If that means your brother making you moan in the shower while I watch, so be it."

"Sounds dirty when you put it like that," I laugh. "I just feel like I should be… I don't know… I never imagined my life without her. Now I have to relearn the world without her in it."

"You don't have to be a weepy mess curled up in the corner sobbing to do that, baby," Remy says. "You do what comes naturally, and we will be right here no matter what."

"It doesn't feel real," I admit. "Nothing feels real... I am suddenly so fucking numb and it scares me."

"What can I do?" he asks.

"Things I don't think my brother wants to be present for," I say. "I need to be able to close my eyes and not imagine my best friend getting fucked to death by a knife because they accidentally kidnapped her instead of me. Her pain and suffering were meant to be mine. I can't get that out of my head."

Remy glances at Cam before turning me to face him. I gasp when he pushes me forward so that my hands are on either side of my brother and I am bent at the waist. "Remy," I say. I try to stand up, but he smacks my ass hard, shutting me up.

"We are going to push some boundaries," Remy says as he kicks my feet apart and slides two fingers into my pussy.

"Fuck," I hiss. Cam's back is against the wall, and he isn't touching me, but my head presses against his abdomen when Remy suddenly starts fucking me with his hand. I moan loudly but try to bite it back when Cam sighs.

"You can't do this, Remy," I groan.

"I can and I am," he says.

"Fuck. Fuck. Fuck," I whimper when he adds a third finger. I open my eyes and something brand new washes over me when I see that Cameron is hard. I slam my fist against the wall in frustration.

Before I can do it again, Cam moves my hands to his waist. Remy grabs me by the hair and pulls my head back as he starts slamming into my G-spot.

"Show him how much of a good girl you are, Lori," Remy says. "Come for us."

"No," I whine.

"You will or I won't stop," he says with a darker tone.

I finally let myself look at Cam, and I hardly recognize the man I am looking at. This is not my sweet older brother. This man... He will be what ruins me. "Fuck, that's good," I moan. He is watching me closely, letting his eyes fall to my chest, my tits are bouncing with every violent thrust that Remy makes. It's when he smirks at me as he lazily strokes his cock that it all hits me at once. My thighs are shaking as my orgasm crashes over me, and Cam's eyes darken with lust.

Fuck, I'm in trouble now.

When Remy lets me stand up, I turn and smack his arm. He laughs and wraps me in a hug. "We love you more than anything in this world, Little Fawn," Remy says as he lifts my chin.

"I love you guys too," I say. "That was... mean."

"I think that was meaner to Cam," he says with a smile. "I am going to make you some tea tonight, okay?"

"Like... Your tea or my tea?" I ask, and he laughs.

"Which would you prefer?"

"Definitely yours," I say.

"If I make you mine, I am absolutely fucking you in your sleep," he says. "Truly depraved things will happen to you."

"Okay," I smile.

"Get dried off and go lie down," he says. "I'll go make tea."

"I'll be out in a minute," Cam says when we go to step out.

"Have fun jerking off in the shower, Cam," I say playfully.

"Watch it. I'll corner you and make you watch," he threatens.

"Yeah, okay," I laugh. I yelp when he suddenly grabs me by the hair and pulls my head back to look at him.

"Right now is not the time you should be a brat to me," he says with a dark tone of voice. "I will break every goddamn boundary to teach you a lesson. Understand?"

"Yes," I say with a small smile. He grunts and releases me. This time I wait until I am out of the shower to be a smart ass. "Was it the tits or the moaning that did it for you?"

"Both," he says simply, shutting the shower door. I am taken aback by his statement, and Remy laughs when I just stare at the shower door for a moment.

Eventually, I dry off and put on a pair of panties and a shirt that Remy gives me I go lie in bed as Remy goes downstairs to the kitchen. I lay in silence and I start worrying about Cameron. He is still in the shower, and he never takes this long in the shower. I might be about to walk in on him jerking off, but he might also need help. His girlfriend was just brutally murdered, so I can't imagine what's going through his head right now.

I get up and slowly open the bathroom door. "Cam?" I say carefully.

"Yeah," he chokes out.

"You good?"

"Yeah, I'm okay," he says, his voice trembling. I step in and open the shower door. My heart breaks all over again when I see him sitting with his back against the wall, crying. I shut the water off and go down to my knees so I can sit back on my heels.

"Cameron," I say softly, putting my hands out for him to take.

"She's gone," he says tearfully. "She suffered and I couldn't save her."

"I know," I say, trying to swallow my tears. "I'm sorry, Cameron. She didn't deserve that."

"Please don't blame yourself," he sniffs. "I can't lose you too, Lori. I can't. I'm afraid I won't be able to save you."

"I'm not going anywhere," I sniff. "We will get through this together. I promise we will."

I pull him toward me and hug him against my chest. He wraps his arms around my waist, and his body shakes as his cries echo through the bathroom. I rock us side to side as I rest my cheek on his head. I sense that someone is behind me, and I look back to see Remy is with us. He leans down and kisses my forehead, snapping Cam out of his depressed daze.

When Cam sits and rubs his hands down his face, I stand and back up so he can. "I'm sorry. I..."

"Shut up," I say, handing him a towel. "Don't apologize to me for having emotions. We all lost Beatris today, and you have just as much right to those feelings as I do."

"I just... I fucking hate that she suffered," Cam says as he steps out of the shower and dries off.

"We all know her stubborn ass was doing anything she could to piss the fucker off," Remy says, making Cam and me smile.

"She lived to piss people off for fun," I say.

"You and her both," Cam adds with a smile.

"Move in with us," Remy says to Cam. Cam looks from him, to me, and back to him before answering.

"Are you sure?" he asks.

"Absolutely. I know you don't want to go back to the home you were supposed to share with Tris, and I think you two would heal better together than in different houses," Remy says. "Also, I think it would help Lori a lot to have us both in the same house."

"Nothing will make that better unless I have both of you right beside me," I say with a sigh.

"Well, at least for now, he can sleep up here with us," Remy says.

"I have mixed feelings," I laugh.

"Don't wanna snuggle with both of us?" Remy asks with a playful smile.

"It's not that. I will still want to get fucked. I don't know how that is supposed to happen if Cam is sleeping next to me," I laugh.

"Same as before, only we'd have an audience," Remy winks. I look at Cam, and he grins at me as he pulls on shorts. I shake my head at him before stepping past him and going into the bedroom. I spot my tea on the bedside table and smile.

"Wait, are you really drugging her?" Cam asks.

"I asked him to," I say. "I don't picture myself falling asleep on my own, and I know I need it. We all do."

"Don't drink just yet. I ordered pizza," Remy says. "Start a movie and I'll go grab it."

"Mkay," I say. I move to sit in the center of the bed with my back against the headboard and Cam sits beside me. I lay my head on his shoulder, and he relaxes. "Can I ask you something I probably shouldn't?"

"You can," he chuckles.

"Why were you... hard?" I ask.

"Because you are a beautiful woman, Lorelei," he says almost cautiously.

"I was super afraid you were about to jerk off in my face," I say.

"That would have been funny," he laughs.

"If you came in my face?" I ask, laughing with him. "That shit hurts if it gets in your eyes."

"Noted. Not in the face," he says.

"There is a lot more here that we should probably talk about one day," I say.

"I get the feeling I'm going to be left out in the cold when you two end up snuggling," Remy says when he comes into the room with pizza in hand.

"See, that's when you just snuggle up with us and sandwich me," I say. Remy raises an eyebrow at me and my face heats with a blush. "I... didn't mean that the way you just took it."

"Yeah, you did. That's okay," Remy laughs. "You didn't start a movie."

"Oh yeah," I say. I lean over Cam and grab the remote as Remy sits beside me. I start searching for something to watch that won't remind us of Tris and land on a random TV show. I focus on my food and not on the television. It doesn't get far before I push my food away and sit back.

"You need to eat," Cam says.

"I can't," I say. "I tried, and I can't."

"I'll make you a deal," he says. "Finish the slice you started, and I'll leave it alone."

"Okay," I sigh. I pick up my half-eaten slice and eat the rest before tossing the crust down. "Can I have my tea now?"

"Yeah," Remy says. He hands me my cup and my eReader before closing up the pizza box and moving it so I can stretch my feet out. I drink my tea faster than usual as I get my book loaded up, and Remy just watches me.

"What?" I ask.

"That shit is going to hit you hard," he warns. "You are drinking that way too fast, and I put more than normal."

"More sleep for me," I say, taking the last sip. He takes the cup, and I move down to lie on the bed, and Cam does the same. I am turned slightly so Cam cannot see what I am reading. Remy lies down, and I assume he is on his phone until he whispers in my ear.

"Naughty girl... I should have known you'd be reading something like that," he says before gently kissing my neck, just below my ear. I am reading a book about a girl who fucks her brother and his best friend. Once again, I'd be a damn liar if I said I wasn't living vicariously through these characters. I go to lock the eReader, and he stops me. "No, keep reading. I want to know what the brother does next."

"I'm sorry?" Cam says as he rolls to face me. My face heats up, and Cam grins at me. "What are you reading, Lori?"

"Nothing," I laugh. I try to wiggle away when he slides his arm under me and pulls me to his chest before taking the eReader. Remy moves in close behind me, propped up on his elbow with his hand on my hip.

"What do we have here?" Cam says as he starts reading the scene I am on, which happens to be her getting absolutely railed by her brother for the first time.

"Cam," I whine and try to reach for it. "I'm getting too tired to fight you."

He holds it out so I can't reach it, but eventually I get too tired to keep my arm up, so I lay my arm on his chest. My palm is flat against his skin, and I can feel the way his muscles tense as he reads. He turns his head and looks at me, and I can't help but laugh at the look on his face. "You dirty girl. You read this stuff?"

"Yeah," I say with a blush. I try to hide my face, but he lifts my chin.

"Who knew my pretty little sister had a filthy mind," he says sweetly before whispering his next words. "Just like me."

"It's bad," I mumble.

"Why do you read about siblings?"

"If I can't do it, may as well read about it," I mutter, or at least I think I do. I can't keep my eyes open my more, so I let them close. Cam gently kisses my forehead before letting me lay my head on his shoulder. I am surrounded by the both of them, and I feel safe. I have to believe that her death was for a reason. I have to hold on to hope that there is sunshine behind the clouds that currently loom over us.

Chapter Sixteen
Remington

I AM PROPPED UP on my elbow, watching as Cameron holds Lorelei in his arms. They both need this. I need to see this. I've known for a long time that he loves Lori in ways that maybe a brother shouldn't. We share the same darkness, so it's natural that we'd gravitate toward the same woman. I know he loved Tris. It's not like he was settling with her because he couldn't, or felt like he couldn't, have Lori; he truly loved her.

I'm surprised he hasn't mentioned it, but Lori had said she remembered seeing Cam in her dorm room jerking off to Tris sleeping, but it was definitely her that he was jerking off to. It was Lori that he was touching. I know this because I was hiding, waiting for him to leave. I had drugged them both so I could play with Lori, and he showed up.

They're both adults, and as long as he doesn't knock her up with an inbred baby, who cares? Why can't they make their own decisions? Having him live here is perfect because no one would suspect anything. We have a room set up with his clothes and belongings in it, but we will stay in here. Hell, we can put a king-sized bed in both and sleep wherever.

"She asleep?" I ask.

"I think so," he says. "How can you tell?"

I roll Lori to her back, and she lets out a sigh, but is definitely asleep. I pull one eyelid open for a second to see if she will react, but she doesn't. "She's out," I say. "She will be for at least a few hours. I gave her a lot, so she should sleep pretty hard until morning."

"Is that safe?" he asks softly.

"Yes, it's safe," I laugh. "You don't have to talk quietly. You're definitely not going to wake her."

"How are you doing with all of this?" he asks.

"Well," I say. "I loved Tris like a sister. She was an incredible woman, and she didn't deserve that, but I am hyper-focused on Lori. I'm scared someone will take her and even more so now that we know what they'd do."

"I won't survive if I lose her, Rem," he says seriously. "This woman right here is the only thing keeping me grounded and I can't lose her."

"You won't," I say. "We just need to be vigilant."

"Yeah," he sighs.

"Wanna talk about what happened in the shower?" I ask.

"Which part?" he asks, and I laugh.

"I assume I know why you were upset, but let's start with the first thing," I say. "I tested you two to see if she would stop it from happening and if you would allow it. Not only did you allow it, but you got hard."

"Yeah," he says simply. "Now, I assume the realization that you get hard for you sister brought up some guilt, which led to the breakdown."

"Yeah…"

"Did Tris know?" I ask.

"Yeah," he sighs. "She knew."

"Care to explain it to me?" I ask.

"Rem," he sighs.

"Dude, you had your hard dick *in her face*, and neither of you even flinched. You think I would do something like that and then get mad when you tell me exactly what I have known for years?" I ask. "Also, for the record, when she mentioned her catching you jerking off touching Tris, I know the truth behind that. You interrupted me trying to play with her, but I got to see you play with Lori instead."

"I... where were you?"

"The closet," I laugh. "Tell me the truth. It's me, Cameron."

"I am in love with Lorelei," he says as he watches her sleep. "I have tried so hard to stuff it down and not say anything .. I finally told Tris last night, and she was so happy... Tris planned on telling her tonight for me."

"Fuck, I'm sorry, man," I say.

"I don't know how to explain it, but it's like I knew that she was going to die," he says. "It felt like she just wasn't meant for this world. It just hurts so goddamn bad that she suffered. All of this makes me feel guilty."

"You have nothing to feel guilty for," I tell him. "If you did, you know I'd say something."

"I know," he sighs. "I don't know what to do."

"What do you want to do?"

"The very toxic side of me wants to fuck her in her sleep," he says.

"Then do it," I say. "I told her that I would fuck her in her sleep and filthy things would happen to her body. I think getting fucked by her brother qualifies as filthy."

"You are a bad influence," he says, and I laugh.

"What are the odds that a woman asks to be drugged so she can sleep, but also be played with?" I ask. "She happily fell asleep in your arms after she just sat and admitted to wanting to fuck you."

"What if she wakes and freaks out?"

"She won't and if she did wake, she wouldn't freak out," I say. "How about this? I am going to do what she already knows I am going to do, and then I am going to go to the basement and set up this pole for her so she can have that escape. You will be free to do whatever you want."

"Okay," he says.

"She isn't on birth control, by the way," I tell him.

"I got a vasectomy years ago," he says. "Tris and I talked about that last night."

"You did? Why?" I ask.

"Because I knew one day, I was going to fuck my little sister, and I didn't want to chance getting her pregnant," he says with a smirk. "Tris and I would have just ended up adopting. Now…"

"Now, we just wait until your parents die, I knock her up, and we both get to be dad," I say, and he laughs.

I pull the covers off Lori and undress her. Cameron watches intently, but looks like he is going to explode if he doesn't touch her titties. "Go on," I say. "Her body will react, but she will stay asleep."

He is hesitant, but gently cups her breast, lightly squeezing. When he pinches her nipple, she gasps softly in her sleep. A smile spreads across his face, and he does it harder. Same reaction, but she stays fast asleep. When he leans down and starts sucking and biting her nipples, a beautiful moan spills out of her.

Satisfied that he is happy, I spread her legs and dip my head to lick across her already swollen clit. "Fuck, she is soaked," I murmur.

"She is?" he asks.

"Mhmm. That was all you," I tell him. When I drop my head and push my tongue inside of her.

"Fuck, this woman will be the death of me," Cameron groans as he frees his cock.

"Save it for her," I say, glancing up at him. "Deny yourself now so she can have it all later."

"Can she come in her sleep?" he asks.

"Absolutely. Watch."

I suck on her clit and more moans sound through the room. I slide three fingers into her cunt and curl them as I continue sucking hard. Her body is trembling, and I know it won't take much more. Her pussy has a fucking vice grip on me, and she is panting as she nears her orgasm. When it breaks, the most incredible moan comes out of her, followed by a whimper.

"Fuck, that's hot," Cameron grunts. I move up to kneel between her legs and his eyes go wide. "You really are going to fuck her?"

"Dude, it's been my dream to fuck this girl in her sleep for a really long time," I say as I hook one limp leg with my arm. I free my cock with my other hand before hooking the other leg and leaning into her. She whimpers when I slam into her cunt, but instantly grips onto me as I start to fuck her. "Fuuuuck, that's so good."

I let myself get lost in this feeling and start pounding into her, only focused on getting myself off. Her body reacts by squeezing and releasing my cock, and the cutest whimpers and moans come out of her. She never even so much as flutters an eyelid. My balls start to tighten, and I am grunting and growling as I keep fucking her until I finally come. My body shudders as I fill her. When I pull out of her cunt, I am still painfully hard. I am still soaked in her come, so I gently slide into her ass.

"Fuuuck," I groan. "Shit, she is so fucking tight, man."

"Dear God, you are in her ass," Cameron groans.

"She feels like fucking heaven," I say. I can already feel myself on edge, so I make the most of it by rapidly quickening my pace and fucking her as hard and deep as I can. I don't last long in her ass before I explode inside of her again.

Satisfied with how I have filled her, I pull out and back off. Her legs are spread open and my come is dripping out of her. Lori's breathing is returning to normal, but her muscles are still trembling from the aftershock of her orgasms.

"She is all yours; like a wet and ready fuck toy that moans when you bottom out," I say.

Chapter Seventeen
Cameron

I WATCH AS REMINGTON walks out of the room, leaving me with my drugged, unconscious sister. She is full of his come and as fucked up as this is, I want to eat her clean and then fuck mine into her. I watch her sleep for a moment, but I am so goddamn hard that I just can't help myself. I need to know what they taste like; my sweet little sister and my best friend.

I move between her legs and spread her wide open so I can push my tongue into her cunt. Her entire body shudders and I groan against her pussy. Fuck, they taste amazing. It's like a sudden addiction and I am desperately swirling my tongue inside of her, cleaning his come out of her. The sweet little moans she makes when I suck him out of her send bolts of pleasure straight to my cock. I swear to God; I could come from this alone.

I lift her hips and repeat the process to clean her. She is so goddamn sensitive that she even mewls when I clean him out of her ass.

When every drop of his is gone and she is trembling on the edge of an orgasm, I move up. I grab the back of her knees and push them to her chest before spreading them wide so I can watch and I force my cock into my little sister.

"Fuck," I groan. "This is so wrong... but I need you so badly; as much as I need air to breathe."

I slowly fuck her, watching as I bury deep and slowly pull out. It's like magic how her petite body can swallow my thick cock. I am not small. For a long time, I thought my nearly ten-inch cock was a normal size, but it's not. The girth is what stretches her so beautifully. I can see the way her body struggles to fit me, and it's like a drug. Remington is big too, but a bit smaller.

I quicken my pace and push deeper, making her whine in her sleep. I can't stop, even at the risk of waking her. Soon I am pounding into her, lost in the heavenly feeling of her cunt gripping me. I can feel the way the walls of her pussy flutter around my cock, and I want to come so badly. I look down at my beautiful sister as I desperately fuck her sleeping body and thank every fucking star in the sky for her existence.

I can see her hands are weakly gripping onto my wrists as I rail into her. If she is awake, it's hardly at all. I am fucking her so hard that there is no way she won't feel this in the morning. My balls tighten, and just as I am about to come, her beautiful eyes flutter open for just a moment as she is mid orgasm, muttering the most perfect words. "God, I love you, Cam," she mutters.

"Fuck!" I groan loudly as I slam deep to drain my cock inside her. She is already fast asleep again by the time I pull out.

"Well, goddamn, Cameron," Remington chuckles from behind me. "She's going to be feeling you for days."

"That's the idea," I laugh breathlessly and I move to lay beside her and collect my thoughts. Remington cleans her, but leaves her undressed as he gets into bed with us.

"So?" he asks.

"I am one hundred percent going to hell," I say, and he laughs. "She definitely woke up for a second."

"See if she remembers it in the morning," he says. "Don't offer the information, but tell her the truth if she asks. I'm not going to give her a step by step, but I will be open about her getting fucked multiple times."

"Of all people… Why did I have to fall in love with her?" I ask.

"The universe has a sick way of showing its humor, I guess," he says. "When it's just us three, don't be afraid to push her. She can handle it and will very much speak up if she is uncomfortable."

"I'm going to do that again… and again… eventually I'll do it when she's awake," I say. "She is addicting."

"Don't I fucking know it," he laughs.

Chapter Eighteen
Lorelei

Gentle kisses on my face pull me out of my sleep. When I open my eyes, I find a smiling Remington. "Good morning, pretty girl," he says, kissing my lips.

"Morning," I mutter.

"Sleep okay?"

"Yeah, although I am sore in special places. Have fun?" I ask.

"Lots of fun," he laughs. I sit up and rub my hands down my face. "Cameron is making coffee."

"What time is it?" I ask.

"Nine. I sent an email out to all the staff for a mandatory meeting at ten, including those working remotely. I sent the clients and board members the same email. Andrea called a press conference at the office. We will talk to everyone inside first, then we will do the press conference after," he says.

"I could have done that," I say. "Thank you."

"No problem," he smiles. "After, we can go up to the funeral home and plan the service to get that out of the way. When all of that is done, I have a surprise for you."

"Oh?" I ask. "What is it?"

"It wouldn't be a surprise if I told you now, would it?"

"Right," I laugh and get out of bed.

"I also picked you out an outfit for today," he says, pointing to the chair. I walk over and hug him and he lifts my chin to kiss me.

"Thank you," I say. "It's so helpful to not have to think about these things."

"Anything I can do to make things easier, I will," he says.

Once I get dressed, I pull my hair up into a ponytail, so I don't have to deal with it, and we go downstairs. I don't bother with makeup because I will inevitably cry and ruin it anyhow.

"Morning," Cam says as he hugs me as soon as I get into the kitchen. I hold on to him for a moment when reality sinks in that she is, in fact, not here. I sniff back my tears back pull away to wipe my face.

"I'm sorry. I don't know where that came from," I say.

"What happened?" he asks softly.

"I just... I expected her to be sitting here with a smile on her face," I say. "Sleep okay?"

"Yeah," he smiles. "It was easier with you two there."

"Morning," Ross says from the doorway to the kitchen. I turn and see that Andrea is with him.

"Hey," I sigh.

"You look like you just woke up," Remy laughs.

"Mmm. Yeah. I had another officer with me, so someone was watching out," he says.

"So... Beatris' autopsy was completed last night," Andrea says.

"Oh?" I ask. "And?"

"How blunt do you want me to be?" she asks.

"I want to know the truth," I say.

"She was whipped and sustained significant welting and bruising from that. She has a large bite taken out of the tip of her shoulder, but the piece was not recovered. Her clitoris was cut off and found in her stomach contents. The most significant injury was from a large knife that she was assaulted with. It damaged her cervix, uterus, intestines, and severed major arteries. She lost a significant portion of her blood, so death happened within minutes of those injuries. Semen was found in the abdominal cavity, so it's likely that she was assaulted at death or after," she says bluntly. "Start to finish, the medical examiner estimates that the entire interaction would have taken no more than thirty minutes. The severity of the injuries occurred in the last few minutes, in my opinion."

"So... he whipped her, cut her clit off, fed it to her, ate a chunk of her shoulder, fucked her with a knife, then fucked her dying or dead body?" I ask.

"Yes," Andrea says.

"Well, goddamn," I say, huffing out a dry laugh.

"She suffered, but it wasn't for long," Ross says. "That's what this boils down to."

"Also, the medical examiner said that she likely went into shock very early on because the bite in her shoulder and her clitoris being removed caused massive blood loss also, so there is a good chance she didn't feel a lot of it, or she was unconscious," Andrea says.

"Well... that makes me feel a bit better," I say. "What the fuck is wrong with humans? Who decides to do shit like this?"

"Monsters," Ross says.

"Well," Cam says. "Definitely not repeating that in any meetings today."

"Shit. Tris would want me to, just to freak people out," I say, and he laughs. "I am learning that trauma makes me say inappropriate things."

"Sometimes we have to laugh through the pain, or it will eat us alive," Ross says.

"Kinda like her eating her clit," I say, making Remy laugh this time. "Ignore me getting it out of my system before I get to the office."

"Don't feel bad for how you cope," Ross says. "There is no correct way to handle this."

"I think us being together helps a lot," I say. "If I was isolated… I would be batty by now."

"We should get going," Andrea smiles.

"When will her body be released?" I ask as I grab my bag.

"Oh, it's going to be a while longer. We want to keep her body for a little bit so we can make sure we have every bit of evidence," she says. "DNA will take a while to come back. Hopefully, the asshole is in the system and gives himself up that way."

"Mmm. That would be too easy," I say. "Someone like this is far too calculated and meticulous to leave something behind that would get him caught."

"Unfortunately, you might be right," Ross says. "But we have plenty of other leads to follow."

We pull into the parking lot, and everyone comes around to me. I walk between Cam and Remy and none of us stop, because if we do, we might not ever walk in there. When we stop in front of the building, I decide we should just tell the media. We are already here, and they are waiting.

"Andrea," I say. "Can we…"

"Yeah," she smiles. "If you can't… I'll take over. Just say what you can, but absolutely do not mention the connection to human trafficking or that you were the target. Okay?"

"Okay," I sniff.

"Quiet everyone," Andrea calls out. A hush falls over everyone, and I am already fighting back tears.

"Good morning… I am Lorelei Belmont," I say, my bottom lip quivering. "I uh… we promised updates… I'm sorry."

I stop and take a deep breath and luckily, they are all patient with me. I can't choke back the tears, though. Instead of stopping them, I just let myself cry. "Yesterday afternoon… Our friend and newly appointed COO, Beatris Cooper… She left the office to get everyone lunch, but she uh… shit. I'm sorry."

"It's okay. Hey. I've got it," Andrea says, rubbing my back. "Thank you for being patient, everyone. Beatris Cooper was abducted on her way back. A little under three hours later, she was found deceased. This was a violent attack, and we are actively following several leads. We ask that if anyone has any information to reach out to their local precinct, and we will look at every single one. This is not considered a public threat, but we do ask that everyone remain vigilant. Thank you."

We are quickly taken inside before anyone can ask anything. I immediately turn and hug Remy before I completely fall apart. He hugs me tightly and I fight back sobs. When I pull away, I hug Cam.

"Hey," I hear Sam sniff nearby. He is the only one who knows.

"Hey," I say tearfully when I pull away. "I'm sorry. I'm trying not to."

"Stop. It's fine," Sam says as he hugs me. "I'm so sorry, Lori."

"I hate this so much," I whisper.

"I know," he sighs. "So do I."

"I don't know how I'm going to get through this," I say as I pull away.

"One step at a time," he says. "Everyone is watching us, though."

"Right. All staff," I sigh. I glance and see that everyone is confused by this. "Hey, everyone. Uh... floor leads. Do we have everyone?"

"Yes," a few say.

"I went ahead and did attendance," Sam says, handing me a tablet. "Also, the board and all the clients are here."

"God, you're a saint," I say. "Thank you, Sam."

"I am going to make you guys let me help you. Use me however you need. Okay?" he asks.

"She will," Remy says before I can answer.

"What's going on?" Leann asks hesitantly. I sigh and turn to everyone.

"I can't promise that I won't break down. I am hardly hanging on here, so please be patient," I say before taking a deep breath. "Yesterday, Tris left the office to get us lunch while we prepped for the all-staff meeting. The plan was for us to meet up with her after the meeting to eat... On her way back, she was abducted... By the time we got out of the meeting, she had been found dead."

Gasps break out across the room, but it's Matthew that catches my attention. Tears roll down his face and he looks *guilty*.

"I will give you all a little bit better of an explanation than the media was told, but I'm not going into detail," I continue. "Tris was violently killed. She suffered and she did not deserve that... Tris was kind and incredibly smart. We've known her our entire lives and she meant the world to us... Her autopsy was completed last night, but her body won't be released for a while. I am planning her service today and I want everyone to know that you *are* invited. I know that she meant a lot to many of you. She was more than just a manager here. She lit up this building with her sarcasm and bright, bubbly nature... She absolutely loved working here and I know her presence will be sorely missed. Sam will be taking over her duties and helping us where needed... We will still be here because we still have a company to run... if anyone knows me, though, I hate delegating, and I would rather do everything myself, but I can't. I can't manage everything alone right now, so please go to Sam if you need anything. If it is absolutely detrimental, we will be here."

"To the board members and our clients, please know that this is not going to affect anything. Everything will continue as planned. For right now, we are not replacing the COO position, but Sam seems to be sneaking his way into those duties, though."

"Kinda bulldozing my way in," Sam says with a smile. "Guys, despite what she has said, do not go to them. Come to me and I will handle everything and update them as needed. Cameron and Remington are a bit more compliant with this, but we all know Lorelei will not be... She is very much going to try to continue to run everything, but this is the time where we need to think about her as a person rather than our boss. Cameron and Remington know that I am making this... decision, if you will... next week, they will be traveling for a meeting in..."

"No location," Andrea interrupting.

"Ah. Right. They won't be in town for this meeting, so I don't want anyone to worry if you don't see them around the office... Cameron and Remington are going to try to keep her out of this office and work from home, but I think that's a battle we will all lose," Sam adds.

"I feel like I should be offended," I say, and everyone smiles despite the tears. "I know that whenever bosses say that we are like a family, it's usually bullshit, but you guys are my family. Many of you have been here since the very beginning and I can't even begin to explain how thankful we are for you guys... Andrea?"

"We will be asking every biological male employee in this building to submit a DNA sample," Andrea says. "This is not required, but I will be transparent and say that if you refuse, I will just get a warrant... Even despite having an alibi, Cameron and Remington have submitted DNA. We can obviously rule most of you out based on camera footage during the meeting, but not everyone. This is not to say that someone here is guilty because I don't think it's anyone in this building, but I do want to do the due diligence of checking... I will be here with a few officers to collect through today."

"I will send everyone an email with the memorial information for Tris later today," I say. "I will make sure that it is outside of normal work hours, for obvious reasons. I know this is a hard hit for everyone, so please just do your best. If you need support, I highly encourage you to reach out to us, but we will also have numbers available for you all to talk to counselors if needed."

"Do you have any questions?" Cam asks.

"How... How did she die?" a girl asks. I look at Andrea and she speaks up.

"Tris was sexually assaulted," Andrea says. "This violent attack caused life-threatening injuries that resulted in massive blood loss."

"Oh my God," Leann says through tears. "Is Lorelei at risk? Is this related to..."

"Lorelei, Cameron, and Remington have around the clock guard. They will never be alone, so no one has to worry about their safety," Andrea says vaguely.

"I'm going to come with you all to the funeral home," Ross says quietly, and I nod.

"Try to have a good day, everyone," I say.

"I am going to have lunch catered so no one has to leave for lunch," Cameron says. "We will also be hiring security, so expect some changes to occur over the next week."

As everyone leaves, Matthew hangs back. "Hey, Matthew," I say. "Are you okay?"

"I feel responsible," he sniffs. "If I hadn't…"

"It was bound to happen to someone," I say. "It's not your fault."

"I am so sorry, guys. Truly. I didn't mean…"

"You didn't kill her, Matthew," I say. "You were in this building when she was taken."

"I'll still submit DNA," he says.

"Just for the sake of reports, we do need to sit down tomorrow and talk," Andrea says.

"Uh. Okay," he says. "I need to go work on this audit still, I guess…"

"Try to have a good day, Matthew," I say. "Don't be too hard on yourself."

Matthew nods and walks away, and I sigh. "Think he had anything to do with it?" Cam asks Andrea.

"No, but I think he knows something," she says honestly. "Let me handle it… I'm serious."

"We have enough to worry about than waterboarding poor Matthew for answers," I say.

Chapter Nineteen

Lorelei

TOMORROW IS THE FUNERAL, but today we have actual work to do. We are on our way to meet with Matthew about the audit. I'm not sure if he is done, but we are worried about him. He had a meeting with Andrea this morning, but she hasn't said anything. We know there are things they can't tell us, so we will try to be patient. If he isn't in jail, I assume he is innocent.

"Ready?" I ask Ross as he types on his phone.

"Uh... yeah. Ready. Sorry," he says. He gets out with Cam and Remy and walks around to my door. They have a habit of this and I just let it happen. It makes us all feel better.

I get out and we all walk to the door. Right away, Ross is on edge when the door is open slightly. "Why is his office open?" I ask as I push the door open.

"Lori, wait," Ross practically yells at me as he looks into the window. It's too late though, as soon as I open the door, I can see straight into his office through the waiting room. The scream that comes out of me is shrill. I jump back and cover my mouth, not believing what I'm looking at.

"Dispatch, this is Detective Yotes. Send a unit to 15th and Collier... Yes, notify the sergeant... Thanks," Ross says into his phone. "Guys, back up."

"What the fuck is happening?" I say as Remy hugs me tightly. Inside Matthew's office, he is hanging by a rope. His eyes are practically popping out of his head, and it looks like he's been there for a minute.

"I am going to clear the building, I need for you three to stay here. Okay? I mean it. Do not move," Ross says.

"We are good," Cam says as he hugs me next.

"He killed himself," I say when Ross walks into the office.

"He felt guilty," Cam says. "Sometimes people can't see past the darkness."

"Why didn't he just ask for help?" I sniff.

"Sometimes people don't want help," Remy tells me as he rubs my back.

"Yeah, just him," Ross sighs and pulls off his gloves.

"He leave a note?" Cam asks.

"Uh. Yeah. It's on his desk. It just says, "I'm sorry, Beatris," and his signature under it," Ross tells us. "When units get here, we can go back to the office, if you want."

"Yeah. We have some paperwork to do," I say. "I need to get lost in that for a while."

"We still have a surprise for you," Remy says, kissing me.

I'VE SPENT THE AFTERNOON doing paperwork. Everyone has left me alone so I can focus. When it hit five, Cam and Remy came into my office and took my laptop. Now, we are pulling into the driveway and the guys are excited. Why? I don't know. I just want to take a scalding shower, but they won't let me do that either.

"Do I need an escort, or can I get out?" I say with an attitude. When no one answers, I scoff and get out.

"Lori," Cam says. I ignore him and go inside. I toss my bag on the couch.

"Hey," Remy says, turning me around.

"What?" I snap.

"I'm going to pretend you aren't being a brat," he smirks.

"I don't give a fuck what you do," I say harshly. He nearly growls as he grabs me by the throat and pulls me close. I grin at him and Cam laughs.

"Lose the fucking attitude or the detectives are going to see you get bent over this goddamn counter," Remy growls.

"I didn't see anything," Ross laughs.

"What is wrong?" Remy asks me.

"I'm just overwhelmed," I sigh. "You won't let me cook myself in the shower. Reading doesn't help…"

"What about dancing," he smiles. I gasp and throw my arms around his neck, and he laughs as he picks me up. He sits me on the counter and cups my face. "I told you I would, so I did. It's an escape for you, and I don't want you to feel trapped."

"Dancing?" Ross asks. "Ohhhh…"

"Go get changed and we will take you down," Cam says.

"Okay," I say with a bright smile. I hop down and Ross still looks confused. "What?"

"Just confused," he says.

"Pole dancing is more than just stripping," Andrea laughs. "It's hard."

"How would you know?" Ross asks, raising an eyebrow at her.

"Pays well and college is expensive," she says with a shrug. The wicked grin that comes across Ross' face when his eyes glance over her body is a dead giveaway.

"I'm going to change," I say. I race upstairs and change into spandex shorts, a sports bra, and a drop armhole tank top. When I get back to the kitchen, Remy smiles at me.

"That's more clothing than I expected," he remarks.

"You would know, wouldn't you??" I say.

"Come on," Cam laughs. "You two are welcome to join, since you are staying for dinner."

"I have no idea what I'm getting myself into right now, do I?" Ross says.

"It's not dirty," Andrea laughs. "We'd love to."

We go down to the basement and the right side of the room has mirrors along the wall and a pole mounted in the center. The floor has newly laid flooring and I can tell he spent a lot of time on this. "You did a lot," I say.

"I worked on it the last few nights while you slept," Remy says. He kisses me gently and nudges me toward the pole. "Go on. Pretend we aren't here."

"Okay," I say happily. I go over to the speaker and hook my phone up to it before finding a song. The others grab folding chairs and sit off to one side as I stretch. When I get done, I pull off my shirt and take a deep breath.

"Take it off," Remy hollers. I laugh and throw my shirt at him.

"Please don't," Ross laughs.

"Shhh," I say. When the current song starts to wind down, I prepare for the song I chose.

I approach the pole and make sure it's locked before grabbing a tight hold. I test my weight on it by swinging myself around once. When I am confident that there is no movement, I hook my leg and sling myself around so I can get upside down.

I easily get lost in the music, focusing on my hand placement and keeping myself securely attached to the pole. Nothing about this is provocative or offensive. I treat it like an art, because it is. When I am dancing, the world doesn't exist. No one is after me. No one wants me to hurt me. It's just me and the music. When the third song comes to an end, I am exhausted. I bring myself down to land in a split before moving my legs out in front of me so I can lie back on the floor.

I am breathing heavily, but I am calm. For the first time since before George hurt me... I'm calm. "That was incredible," Remy says as he offers me his hand. I take it and he pulls me up to stand so he can hug me.

"Thank you," I say softly.

"You're welcome, Little Fawn. Anything for you." He kisses me softly, and I turn around to look at everyone. Cam has a strange look on his face, but Ross and Andrea are smiling.

"You are very talented," Ross says. "I didn't realize that takes so much strength."

"Yeah, it's taken a lot of practice," I say.

"Well, I am going to start dinner," Remy says.

"I am going to go take a shower," I say, hoping I can escape everyone. Remy doesn't say anything since the detectives are here, so I go upstairs before I get a lecture on boiling myself.

I start the shower and strip my clothes off while I go to the counter and take my makeup off. I am tired and sweaty now, but I cannot wait to get into the shower. I gasp and jump back when I turn and find Cameron standing in the doorway. "Christ, Cam," I say. I go to get into the shower and he grabs my waist and pulls me to stand in front of him.

"When I check this shower, what will I find?" he asks, almost daring me to lie.

"That it's wet," I say, letting the last word letting pop as I speak. I smile sweetly and try to turn again, but he grabs my throat and pulls me close.

"If that water is hotter than it should be, you and I are going to have a problem," he says, leaning in to whisper in my ear. I smile when he pulls back, so I lean in to whisper in his ear.

"You talk a lot of shit for being my voyeur," I say. The growl that comes out of him is hotter than it should be. I giggle and pull away from him so I can get into the shower. I hold my breath when the hot water blasts me, but I notice that Cam is getting in with me. I quickly turn and adjust the water right as he grabs me by the hair and pulls me back against his chest.

"I am so sick of you challenging me, Lori," he says. "Can't you see that we just want to help you?"

"I do see it," I admit. "I see a lot of things."

"Like what?" he asks, turning me around before backing me into a corner. He has his hands on the wall at my sides and I try my best to not look at his dick.

"Like the way you look at me," I say quietly.

"How do I look at you?"

"The way Remy looks at me," I answer, my voice getting smaller as he stares me down. He is towering over me and so close that I can feel the heat of his body.

"You knew we were going to check on you. Why did you still try to boil yourself?"

"I... Because... It reminds me that I am alive," I admit.

"The pain?"

"No, just how it numbs my mind," I say.

"What else does that for you?"

"Uh..." I laugh.

"Tell me," he encourages, lifting my chin to look at him.

"Orgasms," I say quietly. A devious grin spreads across his face as he pulls the shower head closest to us down.

"Put your foot on the bench," he says. I give him a weird look, and he just points to the bench. After a moment, I do it. He turns the shower head around and it is on the rainfall setting. It feels nice, but I know what he is about to do. "Keep your eyes on me. Understood."

"Cam," I squeak out.

"Unless you are saying no, it can wait," he says. "Are you saying no?"

"No," I whisper.

"Good girl," he smiles. Before I can say anything, he changes the water pattern on the shower head. The jet hits my clit, and I nearly collapse when my eyes roll back. He chuckles and puts my hand over my mouth so I don't make a noise. "That feel good?"

"Mhmm," I moan.

"Better than burning yourself?"

"Mhmm," I say. I whimper when he smiles and fists his cock with his other hand.

"You see what you do to me, Lori?" he asks as he strokes himself. "I shouldn't want this... I shouldn't want to hold you down and fuck you to tears... I'm your big brother, Lori... I'm not supposed to want to have your cunt wrapped around me."

"Cam," I choke out. I am panting, but I am not fucking moving. I am not ruining this because I want him to come.

"What is it, Lori?" he asks, groaning as he quickens his pace. "What is it?"

I whine and bang my head back against the wall. "Damnit, Cameron," I pout when he moves the jet of water.

"Look. At. Me," he speaks. I lift my head to look at him and he moves the jet back, making a moan escape me. "What do you want? It's just me and you."

"I want to...help you," I choke out. He smiles, gently grabbing my hand. He has me wrap my fingers around his cock before covering my hand with his. I tighten my grip, and he groans deeply. I keep eye contact with him as we start to move, stroking his cock. After a second, he moves his hand to cover my mouth. I'm not confused at all when he drops the sprayer and shoves his fingers inside of me.

My eyes roll back, and I moan against his hand when he curls them just right and starts to fuck me with them.

I grab his hip and pull him closer as I quicken my pace. This suddenly turns into a contest to see who can make the other come first. He moves his fingers inside of me and I nearly collapse. I am losing this silent war, and he knows it.

"Look at my slutty little sister... Coming on her big brother's fingers," he taunts. "If you wanted to be my little whore, all you had to say was please, Lori."

"Fuck, Cam," I moan softly. I go to lay my head back and he grabs my face.

"No. Eyes on me, little sister. I want you to know exactly who is making you feel good," he growls. "Now, come for me, Lori."

"It feels so good," I choke. My pussy tightens around him as I grow closer, and he pushes deeper. "Fuck, I'm gonna come."

"That's it. That's my girl," he coaxes. "Come for me, pretty girl. I want it, Lori... There you go. Oh, that's good, baby. So good."

When my orgasm starts to fade, I surprise us both when I push him back and go to my knees. "Lori, I... Oh fuck," he groans when I wrap my lips around his cock and suck. I grab the sprayer and point it at my pussy. When the jet hits my clit, I groan and take him down my throat to suck hard. I focus on the pleasure and take it all out on Cameron. He keeps his hand on my head and watches as I get us both off.

When my orgasm hits me, I groan around his cock and the vibrations send him spiraling into his own. I take him deep and swallow as he drains his cock down my throat.

As soon as I pull away, he pulls me up and pushes me back against the wall. "I am so goddamn addicted to you; I will happily burn in hell knowing I have already enjoyed heaven."

"I... I think I just cheated," I say quietly.

"No, Remy is... a bad influence," he says.

"I am not," Remy says from the shower door. I instantly tear up and Cam steps aside so Remy can get to me. He smiles softly as he takes my face in his hands. "That... was the hottest fucking thing I have ever seen."

"What?" I ask tearfully.

"Something about you on your knees sucking off your big brother does it for me," he says as he picks me up and presses me back against the wall.

"Jesus, why are you so big?!" I groan as he slides his cock into me. I loop my arms around his neck as he starts to drive into me. "Fuck, that's good, Remy."

Cameron watches us and looks hungry. He has a slight smirk playing on his lips and every time our eyes meet, the less I am able to hold back my desire than I once was. I know it's wrong to want my brother. I know I will burn for this, but I don't care.

By the time Remy is about to come, I am a mess. He has moved me to lie on the bench and has my feet on his shoulders so he can drive into me. I am begging him for more because it's the only words I can manage. He groans and pushes deep to drain his cock inside of me.

When he pulls out and starts cleaning me, I am breathing heavily and trying to teach myself how to form words again.

"What happened to the detectives?" I ask.

"They had to take a call. They finished Matthew's autopsy, so they said it'd be a while for that report," Remy says as he pulls me up to stand.

"Oh," I say. "I'm going to go run away now."

"Nope," Remy says, as he grabs my wrists and pulls me under the water. It's hotter than what he would normally put it at, and that makes me smile. Cam starts washing my hair, and I tip my head back and close my eyes.

"Are you going to make me talk?" I ask.

"Not right now," he says. "Just relax."

"The water is nice," I remark after a beat.

"I won't let you boil yourself, but we can meet in the middle," he says. "You understand why, yes?"

"No," I admit.

"Lorelei, scalding yourself like that intentionally as a result of stress is self-harm," he says. "You are intentionally harming yourself as a way of releasing an emotion."

"Oh... I'm sorry," I say quietly.

"Don't apologize for trying to cope, Lorelei," Remy says as he and Cam start washing my body. "What else helps?"

"Getting fucked," I say bluntly, and Cam laughs heartily. I can't help but smile. "It's true. I can't think about all the shitty parts of my life if I am too busy coming. Although... This is only a recent development that I am learning that it helps."

"Anything specific?" Remy asks.

"I like pain... I think," I say, opening my eyes.

"Got it," he says. "I hope you know that I am not judging either of you, Lorelei."

"I should have talked to you before..."

"You have done nothing wrong," Remy interrupts. "Let's go eat dinner, and then we can watch a movie. Okay?"

"Okay," I sigh.

"What?"

"I just... I need... I don't know what is going on or where things are headed, but it needs to be a slow journey," I say. "Please."

"Okay," Remy smiles. "Still doing filthy things to you in your sleep, though."

"Deal. I can't object if I'm asleep."

"That's the spirit!" Remy laughs.

I DECIDED TO DO something that I admittedly might regret. I was with Remy when he made my tea, but when he left the kitchen for a moment, I poured a lot of it out and replaced it with tea without the sedative. This way, I can stay awake. I have been laying here keeping my breathing as slow and even as I can with my eyes closed, and I think I have them fooled.

I want to know what they do when I sleep. I am extremely tired, so I can comfortably sit here without wanting to crawl out of my skin from boredom.

"She asleep?" Cam asks.

"I can't tell," Remy says. "I've been watching her." He has spent years watching me, I might not actually get away with this. He isn't the one I want to do this for, though, and I think he will understand that. "We can give her a little longer. Do you mind locking up?"

"I can do that," Cam says. He gets off the bed and walks out of the room. A few seconds pass and I jump when he calls me out.

"Brat. Why are you lying?" he says, poking me in the side. I open my eyes, and he chuckles. "You look tired."

"I poured most of it out," I say.

"I know. I saw. Why?" he asks.

"I know you aren't the only one playing with me at night," I say. "I want to know, but I don't want the pressure of having to respond to it."

"Okay," he says. "Stay as relaxed as you possibly can. Let your body react naturally, including noises. I'll put you on your belly so it will be easier to fool him."

"Thank you," I say as he rolls me over and undresses me.

"Think you can handle knowing?" he asks, kissing my shoulder blade.

"I need to know I'm not the only crazy one," I say quietly.

"Oh, honey," he laughs. "You are the sanest one in this house... No talking."

I bury my face in my arm and focus on my breathing. I force myself to meditate, almost. "Andrea is asleep, but Ross is awake. They'll switch off in a few hours," Cam says. "She good?"

"Yeah," Remy says. "She's pretty out of it."

"I am honestly shocked by what happened in the shower," Cam says.

"Why? She looks at your dick every time she gets a chance," Remy laughs.

He's not wrong...

"Looking is different than taking it down your throat," Cam says. "Also, holy fuck."

"She is incredible, isn't she?"

"She is," he agrees. "You haven't put her like that before."

"Nope. Figured you could take her ass this time," Remy says.

Ah, yep. That's my punishment for lying. Cameron is going to fucking break me. He is massive and larger than Remy. I can hardly handle Remy, so I know this is going to be brutal. "Are you sure?" Cam asks, almost nervously.

"I am. She's taken me before, so it will help her body get used to you," Remy says. One of them, I assume Remy, pulls my leg up to push something into my pussy. It presses against my g-spot but is also pressing against my clit. "This will help her body relax so it doesn't hurt her."

"I think her and I should sit down and talk soon," Cam says as Remy moves to straddle my legs.

"If she will," Remy says. "You need to, but she is still hung up on you being her brother."

"I mean, that is a massive thing to get hung up on," Cam laughs.

"I get it, but I also see it this way… You are both adults and of sound mind. You had a vasectomy, so there is no risk of you accidentally getting her pregnant. You living with us wouldn't be abnormal and you two have been super close your entire lives. Just keep the PDA behind closed doors and it's none of anyone's business what you two do," Remy says as he puts lube on me and him.

"I just wish Tris had a chance to talk to her. She would have known exactly what to say. They were practically the same person, and I think Tris dying is what is blocking her," Cam explains.

"What do you mean?"

"I'm afraid she feels guilty for letting it happen because I was with Tris and she hasn't even been gone a week," Cam tells him.

"Tris wanted it though."

"She did. She wanted it for a long time, apparently. She was so goddamn excited to talk to Lori about it," Cam sighs.

"Then do right by Tris and talk to her," Remy says. "Let her talk when she is ready, but you find a good time and just tell her how you feel. No bullshit; just be honest. Maybe include that you've been fucking her in her sleep every night."

"Ah, because that will go over so well," Cam says sarcastically.

"I think she will handle it better than you think," Remy says as he leans into me. He forces a groan out of me when he sinks into my ass. "Fuck, she's tight."

The toy inside of me starts buzzing and the outer part lightly suckles on my clit and Remy starts to fuck me slow and deep. I can't help but moan and whimper as he goes harder and faster.

He is moving at a speed that has little to no regard for my comfort, but the toy keeps me in a blissful state. The way he slams into me is making my belly ache, but I know he is truly preparing me for Cameron. He is so thick that it's almost impossible to take him down my throat like I did. I could, but it's not the most comfortable. Remy is grunting as he chases down his orgasm. When he finally catches it, I can feel him explode inside of me.

My entire body is buzzing, and silence is the loudest thing right now. No one is touching me, but I can feel their eyes on me. The toy is turned up and I moan when it starts sucking my clit hard.

What I am not expecting is for Cameron to slam into me, and I immediately give myself away.

"Fuck!" I yell out, making Remington laugh.

"You can't fool me, little sister," he says mockingly in my ear. I whimper in response, and he draws out and slams into me again.

"Fuck, Cam," I whine.

"Why didn't you just talk to me?" he asks, slowly rocking his hips.

"I wanted to know," I say as I move up to my elbows but keep my head down. He slams into me again, and I keep going. "Fuck... I thought I was pressuring you into something... We are all grieving and I feel crazy."

"We are crazy, Lori," Cameron says before kissing my neck. "You had so many chances to talk to either of us, but you lied instead."

"I'm sorry," I complain.

"Mmm. Too late now, pretty girl," he chuckles. "Remember this the next time you want to try and trick me."

"Oh no," I groan.

Cameron leans back and grabs my hips to pull me up on my knees. He dumps more lube on my ass before slamming back into me. This time I scream, and he finds a speed and depth that instantly makes me fight him. I don't say a word, but I desperately try to get away. The more I try to crawl out from under his body, the harder her fucks me. No matter me fighting or the screams coming from me, it feels so goddamn good to be used by him.

Cameron holds me in place as he surges deeper and groans as he drains his cock inside of me. He kisses my back before moving off me. "Oh shit. Blanket," Remy says, slinging the blanket over me. I pull it over my head and curl up when I hear the detectives.

"Fuck, guys," Ross sighs. "You do understand incest is a criminal offense, right?"

"Lorelei," Andrea says. I say nothing and I feel someone sit on the bed beside me. "Hun, we came in because you were screaming. I need to see that you are okay."

I pull the blanket down enough to see her face, and she is trying hard not to smile. "I'm okay," I say.

"What are you thinking, Lorelei?" she asks with a sigh.

"That my brother has a massive dick," I say and Remy cackles. "I'm fine, Andrea."

"Sit up, please," she says. I do and Remy tosses me a shirt. I pull it on and keep the blanket over my lap. Remy and Cam look amused as they come over to sit next to me.

"You can't..." Ross starts to say.

"Why?" I ask.

"Because it's a crime," Ross says.

"Why?" I ask again.

"What if he gets you pregnant?" Andrea asks.

"He can't. He got a vasectomy," I say.

"How can you possibly have a real relationship?" she asks.

"Same as I would with Remy," I say. "People mind their own business and that is that."

"And if people find out?" Ross asks. "The media?"

"Meh," I shrug. "It's legal in New Jersey and Rhode Island."

"Is it really?" Cam asks me.

"Mhmm," I smile.

"How long has this been going on?" Andrea asks.

"About as long as I was screaming," I say, and Cam laughs. "Guys, look… If you want to press the issue, fine. Do whatever you feel like you have to, but we are consenting adults. No kids are involved. Nothing happened as kids. We are fine."

"He's your brother though," Andrea says. "I couldn't imagine having sex with my brother."

"You could if he looked like Cameron," I say, and she finally cracks a smile.

"Please keep your screaming to a minimum," Ross says with a smirk. "We have to check every time, and I could go my entire life without hearing that again and it would still be too soon."

"Okay," I smile. "I have a question."

"Yes?" Ross sighs.

"Comparatively speaking, how wrong is it for you to be fucking your boss?" I ask. He opens his mouth to say something but stops, making Cam, Remy, and me laugh. Andrea smiles at him and he shakes his head. "Wanna know how I knew?"

"How?" Ross asks.

"When she made the comment about being in college and dancing before, it was the way you looked at her," I say. "It's the same way Remington and Cameron look at me."

"I think my boss is a bit different than your brother, Lorelei," he tries to argue.

"Mine is, what... A misdemeanor and maybe a fine? You'd get fired," I say.

"Is she always like this?" Ross asks Remington and Cameron.

"A brat? Oh yeah," Remy laughs. "Your secret is safe with us."

"How did Matthew die?" I ask.

"He was hung," Ross says simply. I can tell he won't say anything else, but I do notice he said he was hung and not that he killed himself. So, another murder? Someone is desperately covering up their tracks.

"Get some sleep, guys," Andrea says. When they go to the door, they stop when I speak.

"Are we good?" I ask.

"Yeah," Andrea says. "It was a surprise, but you all are consenting and safe. If you get caught by anyone else, we didn't know shit. Got it?"

"Got it," I smile. "Thank you."

"Yeah. Yeah," Ross says, waving us off. He cracks a smile and winks before leaving the room, making us all laugh. I turn and hit Cam's arm with a frown.

"Ow! What was that for," he laughs. "You are the one who was screaming."

"I was sleeping and minding my own business," I say but giggle when he shoves me back on the bed and pins my arms above my head as he straddles my body. "I'm sorry I tried to trick you."

"You actually did," he laughs. "I didn't know until you cussed me."

"Well, damn."

"We need to talk about this," he says.

"Is that why you are holding me down?" I ask.

"Yes. Where is your head?"

"I'm going to say this as bluntly as I can… I love you as way more than my brother. You and Remington are my world. I want everything you have to offer, and I don't care how crazy or twisted that makes me look. I don't care that it's forbidden; I just want you. I have spent so long shoving that down and scolding myself when I'd find you attractive or when I'd get happy when I saw you looking at my body… I just want to be happy, and you two make me happy. You can't knock me up, so we can worry about the rest later," I say. "Your turn."

"It's pretty simply, actually," he says. "I love you and I have for as long as I can remember. I have known for a very long time that I wanted you, but I didn't let myself go there. A few times I slipped up and… So, when you woke and thought I was jerking off to Tris… Yeah, that was to you. I had just turned because I thought Tris was awake. Turns out she was and saw that entire thing."

"You and Remington are so similar," I laugh.

"Can you really go without being able to publicly claim me?" I ask. "No biological children?"

"I knew I didn't want kids when I realized I was in love with you," he says. "As long as I can have you behind closed doors, I will happily look like a bachelor for life."

"I wish Tris was here," I say. "I miss her... so much."

"Me too, sweetie," he sighs and moves to the bed beside me.

"I'm not ready to say goodbye," I whisper. "She should be here making incest jokes and making me feel better about this... She was the closest thing to a sister I had... and now she's gone."

"Then we live for her," Cam says, rolling me to face him. Remy moves in behind me and they squish me between their bodies as Cam pulls the blanket over us. "She wouldn't want us to be sad."

"No. I can hear her now: 'Bitch, stop crying over me and look for me in the clouds.' She always said that when she died, she would be the in the clouds, looking down on me," I say.

"I remember that," Cam laughs. "She said she wanted to be able to piss on everyone."

"That girl was something else," Remy chuckles.

"She is with her parents now," I say after a while. Tris' parents died in a car wreck five years ago and it damn near destroyed her. "She missed them so much... She gets to be with them now."

Chapter Twenty
Lorelei

I AM STANDING IN the mirror wearing all black, and it doesn't feel right. This doesn't feel right. She wouldn't want this. I look sad and Tris hated to see me sad. I huff and strip off the dress and toss it on the pile of other dresses I've tried on. Cameron and Remington are dressed and being incredibly patient with me.

"How can we help?" Cam asks.

"Nothing feels right," I say. "Everything is black. She wouldn't want me to wear black."

"Can I show you something?" he asks. "I had Ross get it for me yesterday from the house."

"What?" I ask. Cam leaves the room and comes back a few seconds later with a bright pink dress with a black hem on the bottom that I recognize. I instantly tear up and nod. "This was her favorite dress... I had one too, but I ripped it by accident... She said that seeing me in it made her happy."

"She told me she always had you wear it because it matched your soul," Cam says. "A lot of light, but a little darkness to keep you humble."

Cam helps me put the dress on and it falls down to my knees. As he zips it up, Andrea and Ross walk into the room. "You look beautiful," Andrea says. "Ready?"

"Yeah," I sniff. I go to the closet and step into simple black heels.

"There will be a lot of police there, as well as the media," Ross says. "You three stay together, no matter what. I don't care if it's going to the bathroom; you stay together. One of us will always be with you. Do not go off with any other officer unless we tell you."

"Not trust the cops?" I ask.

"No," Andrea says. "Beatris and Matthew's initial autopsy results were leaked to the press last night, and it came from the police department."

"Oh fuck," I say as we get to the front door.

"This means they are quickly connecting it to human trafficking," she tells me.

"Which means they know I am a target," I add.

"Mhmm. Sometimes, other people try to sneak their way into an investigation and feed off the attention," she says. "The last thing we need is a copycat or for other women to start showing up killed like this."

"Any hit on the DNA?" I ask.

"No, the lab is backed up, but they are working as fast as they can," she sighs. "They are thinking maybe next week when you all are in Seattle."

"That would be good," I say. "Will anyone be with us then?"

"I'm talking to the local police out there but... it's looking like you might be on your own," she sighs. "Other than asking you to cancel, there isn't much we can do."

"Well, we are taking the company jet. No one knows we are going to Seattle, and the people we are having the meeting with understand that no one can know we are there and know it's for a safety reason. Clay has the hotel suite under his name, so no one will know we are there." I say. "We should be good."

"Unless someone tracks the plane," Ross says.

"I can call Clay and see if he can send his out here," Cam says. "We went to high school with him, so he knows about Tris and a little about the situation, so he will understand."

"Okay. Do that and tell no one," Andrea says. "Ready to do this?"

"No, but we have to," I sigh.

We pull up to the community center, and I am suddenly thankful I overestimated attendance. There are so many cars here, but they have a spot up front reserved for us to park. The media are being respectful for a change, but Leann also volunteered to wrangle them, so we didn't have to worry about them getting in the way. She is a sweet woman, but tough as fuck. She has probably already scared at least one of them

Andrea and Ross get out first before Cam does. Cam and Andrea walk around the car to Ross and Remy before he takes my hand and I get out. The media instantly starts snapping pictures, and I try my best to ignore them.

"Hey," Sam says as he walks up. "Practically every employee is here. Leann has threatened to kill half of the media already, and Matthew's wife is also here."

"Fuck," I sigh. "I'll start with her. What's her name?"

"Kate," he says. We all walk with him to a woman standing by herself by the door.

"Hi. Kate?" I ask.

"Yeah," she smiles softly. "You are Lorelei."

"I am. I am so sorry to hear about Matthew," I say. "I can't imagine."

"You can," she says. "Just in a different way. I'm sorry about Beatris. It's been all over the... well, everything."

"Yeah. I am avoiding... everything," I say, making her smile. "Sam said you wanted to talk to me?"

"Yes. I heard that you were one of the ones who found him?"

"Uh. Yeah. We were coming to check in on the audit. He had missed a meeting and we knew he was feeling down about Tris, so we went to go check in with him," I explain.

"I am so sorry you had to see that. He never would have wanted you all to find him like that," she sniffs. "I don't really understand. I talked to him on the phone, and he was sad, but he was planning on him and me sitting down and talking about what happened with the business. I know about the club and everything... I forgave him for that because I wasn't exactly making his life easy, but... We were fine... he was fine... I'm sorry to be doing this today. I should go."

"No. No. No," I say. "Please, don't go. I promise, it's okay. I can understand how suffocating grief can be. You reach out when you can and if this is how you process, so be it. Matthew was a good man."

"They won't confirm if it was a suicide or not," she says, glaring at Andrea.

"Well, I will tell you what I think," I say. "I think he was killed... One, they said his cause of death was that he was hanged and did not specify suicide. Two, if it was suicide, they would just say that. If they aren't, knowing I saw him, then they have reason to believe that he didn't do it."

"I'm with her," Cam says.

"Who would do something like that?" she asks.

"The same person who raped Tris with a knife," I say bluntly. "You are welcome to sit with us, if you'd like."

"Are you sure? I didn't really know her."

"Tris loved adopting people and making them her friend. If she were here, she would have claimed you the moment she saw you standing alone," I say. "Come sit with us."

"Thank you," she says. "I don't know why I came. I just... Wanted to meet you."

"Sometimes we need a little support. We are the ones who can probably relate the most right now," I say. "Come on."

We get closer to the media, and someone shouts a question. "Lorelei! Are you worried you are next?!"

Leann spins around and looks like she is about to punch him, so I walk over and get her attention. "It's okay. I'll talk to them," I say.

"You sure?" Remy asks me.

"Yeah. People are curious," I say. "I won't stand here all day, but I will answer a few questions."

"Are you worried you are next?" the same man asks.

"Well..." I say, looking at Andrea. She nods, so I tell the truth. "I know I was the intended target. I am concerned that someone or someones will get to me, but I am not going to let it consume my life. I will be vigilant, but I won't stop living because of it."

"Are there any suspects?" a woman asks.

"I am not privy to the investigation," I say. "I know the autopsy findings, and that's about it. Our employees were asked to volunteer to submit DNA, but all biological males within the media and surrounding businesses were also asked. As far as I know, everyone did."

"Including Remington and Cameron?" she asks.

"Yes," I say. "They were the first ones. Sam, the man who is stepping into the COO role and helping us keep things straight, was third."

"Everyone who was asked submitted a sample," Andrea says. "We do not have any suspects at this time, but we are following leads."

"If you could say or ask one thing to Beatris' attacker, what would it be?" a man asks.

"Jeez, uh... Well, I would ask what bratty thing she did to piss them off in the end," I say. "If there was one thing about Tris that everyone knew, it was that she was stubborn... I have no doubt that she did whatever she could to piss them off, even knowing she was dying... She likely knew that it was meant to be me, which would have only fueled her stubbornness. She was extremely protective of me."

"That's all for now," Remy says, knowing I am being overly nice right now and won't walk away.

"Thanks," I say when we walk away.

"You're welcome," he says, holding my hand as we walk.

"Hey," I say when we spot Mom.

"Hey, baby," she says, hugging me tightly. "How are you? Are you okay?"

"I'm okay. Just... going day by day," I say before turning to my dad. "Hey, Daddy."

"Hey," he says as he hugs me back, but pulls away. Mom hugs Cam and Remy just as tightly. Dad seems numb almost. He doesn't do well showing emotion.

"You okay, Dad?" I ask.

"Yeah," he says with a half-smile. "It's just hard to believe she's gone. I've just been trying to stay busy."

"When do you two leave?" Cam asks.

"Tonight," Mom says. "I saw her autopsy was leaked."

"Yeah," I say. "I'm kinda okay with that. At least everyone will get to see what kind of fucking deranged psycho we are dealing with."

"You really think she is a target?" Dad asks Andrea.

"Yes," she says. "We are taking a lot of precautions, though."

"They are stuck to me like glue," I laugh. "Especially with Tris being killed, I am not planning on going anywhere without Remy or Cam. And the detectives."

"You can't live your whole life stuck to someone though, hun," Dad says.

"I know, but until I know for sure her killer is caught and I am not in danger, I have no plans of wandering," I say. "I need to mingle. I will see y'all when it starts."

"You still making a speech?" Andrea asks me.

"Yeah," I say. "I love you, guys."

"Love you too, baby," Mom says.

"Love you, kid," Dad says.

We spend the next thirty minutes mingling and talking with everyone from our employees to people we went to school with. I spot Omar and smile at him.

"Hey, pretty girl," he says, hugging me tightly. "I am so sorry about Tris."

"Thanks," I say. "It's... hard. We are managing."

"The media has been up your ass for days," he says.

"Eh. They are good company for when a psycho apparently meant to kill me and not Tris."

"Oh?" he asks.

"Mhmm," I say, rolling my eyes. "It's dumb and complicated, but either way, they'll have a sea of people to go through before they can get close to me."

"I'm glad you have support," he says. "You know you can call me if you need anything."

"I know. Once things die down, you and I should go get coffee," I say.

"I will hold you to it," he smiles.

"There should be an extra seat if you want to sit with us," I say.

"Sure," he says. "Just point me in the direction.

"See the older couple in the front?"

"Uhhh... yeah," he says. "That's my mom and dad. Allison and Ted Belmont. Just tell them your name, and I'm sure they'll recognize it. I've mentioned you."

"Okay," he says. "I'll meet you up there."

We wander a bit more before I end up at the front with Remy and Cam. Andrea and Ross are close but off to the side. They're on high alert and are constantly scanning the room.

After a moment, everyone stops talking and locks at me. "Hi, everyone. Thank you for coming today to celebrate the life of Beatris Cooper. Tris was truly one of a kind and definitely unforgettable. She was the type whose laugh you could remember two weeks later. She had a bright and bubbly personality and could make anyone smile... I have thought about what I could say that would accurately reflect the person she was, but there aren't words to describe just how special she was. She was a daughter, a sister, a best friend, a girlfriend, a boss, and anything anyone needed her to be. Her love language was making others happy, and boy was she good at it... Tris was incredible at her job and treated her employees with kindness and respect, no matter the situation. She was a shoulder to cry on and so much more. I could sit here all day and tell you all the adjectives that describe her, but it won't be enough... She was fiercely protective of me, and I have not a single doubt in my mind that in her final moments she was still doing everything within her power to not only be a brat, but to protect me... She wasn't supposed to die; I was. I will always remember that this should be my funeral, not hers. With that is the reminder that she willingly died so I could continue to have a chance at life. Because she knows I would have done the same thing for her, ten times over. She knew that no matter what, I would have protected her in my final moments...

"She told me once, 'Lori, when I die, look for me in the clouds. When it rains, know that it's me... pissing on everything,'" I say, and laughter breaks out across the room. I point to the large windows, and everyone sees that it is raining now. "No matter how close you were with her or how well you got along, find comfort in knowing that she will always be watching over us... I will live my life in her honor, but I can't wait to see her again someday... If anyone has anything they would like to say, you can..."

A shot rings through the room and chaos erupts. One second, I am standing, and the next, I am flat on my back with Remington and Cameron shielding me. I am in shock, and my body is numb. Remy and Cam pull away, and I realize when Remy grabs my face that I am completely out of it.

"Talk to me, Lori. I need you to speak," Remy says.

"Lorelei," Cam says.

It's Ross' voice that snaps me out of my daze. "How bad is it?"

"It just grazed her. I need something to stop the bleeding, though. She's losing a lot," Cam says.

I look at my arm and see that I am covered in blood. "Woah," I say.

"You want to sit up? They think you're dead," Cam says.

"Help me stand," I say.

"Ambulance is on its way," Ross says. When I stand, everyone claps.

"I know everyone is freaked out, but I need everyone to find a seat. No one is leaving until we get statements," Andrea says.

"Someone shot me," I say.

"They only grazed you because Cam shoved you," Remy says.

"You both shoved her," Ross says. "Lorelei?"

"Hmm?" I ask.

"You look like you're about to pass out," he says. "How do you feel?"

"I... feel... weird," I say.

"Chair. I need a chair," Cam says. Before anyone can move, everything goes dark.

I OPEN MY EYES, and I'm confused for a minute. I look around and see both Remy and Cam sitting beside me with their hand on my leg. I'm at the house, but I'm on the couch. My arm is wrapped. I look up and gasp, seeing Ross looking down at me. I don't expect him to me looking down at me like that. Cam and Remy snap their heads up when they hear me.

"Hey," Cam says. "Are you okay? Are you in pain?"

"Uh…"

"Here, sit up. Slowly this time," Remy says. He helps me sit up and I close my eyes for a second.

"Ross scared me," I mumble.

"My bad," Ross laughs.

"What happened?" I ask, opening my eyes to look at Remy and Cam.

"You passed out," Cam says.

"No shit," I retort.

"Doctor said between emotions and shock from the injury, your brain decided it needed a nap," Remy says. "You passed out and we brought you here. Your mom bandaged your arm. It doesn't need stitches or anything, but she used glue to seal it up."

"Who tried to kill me?" I ask.

"No idea," Cam says with sigh.

"It was a .22 caliber weapon. No one left the building, so it was someone in there. They must have been standing up in the back," Ross says.

"Sneaky fuckers. Thanks for knocking me over," I say. "Any ideas?"

"Anyone seem out of place today?" Ross asks me.

"I'd have to think about it," I say. "Where are Mom and Dad?"

"Right here," Mom says from the kitchen door. She walks over and leans down to hug me tightly. "I'm glad you're okay, baby."

"Me too. I kinda had a feeling something would happen. Things were going too well," I say.

"Hey, kid," Dad sighs as he kisses the top of my head. He looks pissed. I can understand why, considering someone killed the woman who was like a daughter to him and then shot me.

"Hey, Daddy," I say. "You okay?"

"Mmm. Yeah. I'm okay," he smiles.

"Is everyone else okay?" I ask. "No one got hurt?"

"No. Everyone is okay," Cam says.

"Well... I don't know what to do now that someone tried to kill me," I say.

"Just relax and focus on yourself," Remy says. "I'll help you get showered and changed. You're covered in blood."

"I just want to relax," I sigh.

"We are leaving town after a while," Mom says as she hugs me again. "I love you so much, baby girl. Please be safe, okay?"

"I love you too, Momma," I say. "Thank you."

Dad hugs me, and he holds onto me for a second. "I'll be okay, Dad. I have Remy and Cam," I say.

"Be good," he says.

"Love you, Dad."

"Love you too, Pumpkin," he smiles.

Mom and Dad leave, but Ross and Andrea stay. Ross is staring at me, and I ignore it for a minute but eventually say something. "What is your problem?" I ask with a sigh.

"You are hiding something," he says.

"Ross," Andrea says.

"No," Ross says. "What is it?"

"I don't know if it's important or not," I say.

"What is it?" Cam asks.

"Well… Omar wasn't sitting up front. I don't actually know where he was. I just remember that he wasn't up front," I say.

"He was in the back," Andrea says. "We will talk to him."

"Okay," I sigh.

"Come take a shower," Remy says. "You can nap after."

"That sounds good," I yawn.

Chapter Twenty-One
Lorelei

Six Days Later

Today is the first day I am leaving the house after essentially everyone I know seeing me get shot. They know I'm okay, or at least our employees do, because I've been doing my work and sending emails. Mom and Dad are at the hunting cabin without service. Cameron and Remington have been right by my side through the anger, the sadness, and the horrific nightmares. The first night I spent having nightmares of getting shot over and over again. Thrown into the mix were dreams about Tris and how I know she died. The second night I didn't sleep at all, but then they drugged me. This time was different, though. It wasn't for them to be able to play with me while I slept. No, this was because I refused to sleep otherwise.

Today, we are flying to Seattle. Clay sent his company jet to us so that we could send ours to Florida. We paid the pilot to take it and sit for a few days so that it appears that we are somewhere we aren't.

My arm is healing wonderfully. It hurt for a while, but it's manageable now. I got really fucking lucky. Andrea and Ross have questioned Remy and Cam numerous times on how they knew to save me, but they can't seem to figure out why. They understood why they were being questioned, and the best thing any of us can come up with is that they saw the person, but their brain didn't retain anything because they were worried about me.

None of us have had sex all week. I have been so focused on work that by the time they make me stop, I have to go to bed. It's not that I don't want to; I just need to process things. I think they are mostly afraid of hurting me. I plan to break this dry spell while we are in Seattle, though.

Omar has all but disappeared, which tells me he's guilty. It's hard for me to understand why he would shoot me, but it's looking like he did. That leads me to believe he is the one who killed Tris, but again, why? This has been the hardest to understand because he was my friend, or so I thought.

Tris' body was finally released yesterday morning to the funeral home, and they cremated her immediately. Now, I am holding her urn as we pull up to the jet. I decided to take Tris with us because she always wanted to visit the west coast. I plan to spread a little of her ashes here so that part of her will always be here. After I make three memorial necklaces, I will scatter the rest at a later date. We want to move, but we need to decide where. We've considered New Jersey or Rhode Island for obvious reasons, but we are not dead set on anything yet.

"Call if you need anything," Ross says. "Local police know you will be out here, and you have the number for Detective Valerie Thomas. She should check in with you three at some point, but she will be available if anything happens."

"Okay," I say. "Thank you, guys."

"You're welcome. Please, be safe," Andrea says. "Remember, no social media. Nothing online at all to avoid being traced. Use cash and use the burner phone we gave you."

"We got it, Mom," Cam laughs.

"Mhmm," she smiles. "Be good."

"We won't," I smile.

We get out, and the guys get our bags as I carry the urn. When we get on the plane, I place it with the bag in the compartment for luggage. The last thing I want is her ashes opening and going airborne.

"Need anything before we takeoff, guys?" The pilot asks.

"No, we are okay," I say. "Thank you for this."

"Not a problem," he smiles. "We didn't want to have too many people involved, so we only have the pilot and co-pilot. It's easier this way should anything happen. We are intentionally leaving late at night so we will have all day for the meeting."

"Come lie down," Cam says.

"I'm okay," I say. I go to sit, but he grabs me by the throat and pulls me close. "We are in public, Cameron."

"Go, lie down. I'm not asking."

"Bossy," I say.

"Bratty," he retorts. I stick my tongue out at him and while Remy laughs, I yelp when Cam suddenly yanks me forward and nips my tongue.

"You freak," I laugh and playfully smack his chest.

"Sweet little sister," he smiles and gently kisses me. "You let your big brother fuck your ass and *begged* for more. We are both freaks."

"I'll own it," I say with a grin.

"Please go lay down, Lori. You need sleep," he says.

"You need sleep too." I frown.

"We will be in there once we are in the air," he says. "I promise."

"Okay," I sigh.

I go back to the sleeping quarters and strip down to just a t-shirt and panties. By the time I get into bed, the plane starts moving. The bed has a built-in belt, so I fasten that over the top of the covers and close my eyes.

By the time we are in the air, I am almost asleep. I can sense that the guys are in here, but I'm too tired to open my eyes. The belt is taken off and they both get into bed with me before I am pulled against Remy's chest. I snuggle up to him and Cam moves close to me so he can press his chest against my back. They both wrap their arms around me and I fall asleep.

I WAKE SUDDENLY TO the feeling of hands on my thighs. My hands are behind my back and a blanket is wrapped tightly around my abdomen before the belt is pulled tight, keeping me tied to the bed. I lift my head up but groan and let it fall back down when I see Cam smile at me.

"Morning," he smiles.

"Why am I unable to move?" I ask.

"Because I'm about to be mean." He grins. I whine when he kisses up my thigh. Remy lies on the bed beside me and props up on his elbow to look down at me.

"Comfortable?" he asks.

"Mean," I frown. "Why do I have to be restrained?"

"Because he is going to make you come until you call your safe word," he says before kissing me.

"*Evil*!" I say again, but even more dramatically. "Why?"

"To make sure you will actually say it," he says. "It's important that we know you will say it when you need."

"Why?"

"Because we plan to fuck you at the same time in that hotel, and we need to make sure if we overwhelm you that you'll speak up," he clarifies.

"Oh..."

"When you've had enough, say apricot," he says, kissing me again.

"Oh... my God," I groan when Cameron flicks his tongue across my clit.

"You know... that first night. Cameron ate my come out of your pussy and ass?" he says. "You came so pretty for your big brother."

"Oh, that's good," I pant.

"Who's eating that pretty pussy, Lori?"

"Cam."

"Who?" he asks.

"Cameron!"

"Who, Lori?" he asks again.

"Fuck," I whine.

"Say it. Who is eating your pussy, Lorelei?"

"My brother," I moan. "Oh, fuck! My brother is. Jesus, that's good."

Cameron is sucking my clit with three fingers deep in my cunt, moving them around like a goddamn expert. These men know exactly how to play with my body, and I'm in love. God, I am so fucking in love with them. I will happily burn in the hellfire just to let my big brother make me come one more time.

An orgasm suddenly hits me, and I moan, but he doesn't stop. He keeps sucking and biting my clit, pulling orgasms out of me back-to-back. As I move through my pleasure, I become desperate for reprieve.

"I can't. Oh God. Please. Stop. I can't. No more," I beg.

"One more, Lori." Remy smiles.

"Nooo," I whine, and try to wiggle my hips to get away from his mouth. He starts fucking me harder with his hand. My legs are shaking and I am moaning wildly. When it breaks, my arousal floods out of me and Cam growls as he drinks from me. When the feeling fades but he doesn't stop, I call out immediately.

"Peach!" I shout and Remy cackles. "No. Fuck... Fruit... Apricot. Stop it."

Cam and Remy are laughing heartily as I try to catch my breath. "Peach?" Cam asks before kissing me, still amused.

"Let me go, you psycho," I complain.

"And here I was going to be nice when I fucked you," he smirks as he pushes my knees to my chest. Remy covers my mouth with his hand, and I scream into it when Cameron slams into me. My eyes roll back as he starts to pound into me, fucking me to literal tears. No holds barred; he pounds into me like he has a lesson to teach me. It feels amazing in the most painful way. By the time he comes, I can't form words or anything more than a grunt.

Cam replaces Remy's hand and my knees stretch back to my chest so Remy can slam into me. I scream again and shake my head, trying to get him to move his hand. When he does, his words surprise me.

"Go ahead. Beg for mercy," he says mockingly. "Mercy is at our discretion. Go ahead. Say the word."

"Fuck, it hurts," I say tearfully. Despite giving the impression that they will continue regardless of what I say, Remington does slow down. I hear a buzzing sound before Cam presses something to my clit. I gasp and he covers my mouth as a mind-numbing orgasm rips through me. The toy is sucking my clit and vibrating, sending shock waves of pleasure through my body.

"There you go. Good girl," Cam praises. "Relax and let him use your tight little cunt."

Orgasms roll out of me, and I am nearly unconscious by the time Remy pushes deep to drain his cock inside of me. They unwrap me before cleaning my body. By the time they get me dressed, the plane is touching down.

"I'm so tired now," I whine as Remy pulls me up to stand.

"We have a full day of meetings," he says, kissing me.

"Boo," I say.

"Come on," Remy laughs as we walk out of the back room. Once we have the bags and Tris' ashes, Clay steps onto the plane.

"Hey!" I say happily.

"Hey, sweetheart," he says as he hugs me. "I'm so sorry about Tris."

"Hear someone tried to shoot me at her funeral?" I ask.

"Mhmm. They figure it out?"

"No." I frown. "I think I have a guess, though."

"Oh?"

"Someone I worked with at the club. His name is Omar. It doesn't make any sense why he would try to kill me, but it's the only thing that makes sense. He disappeared right before I was shot and was in the back. I've also tried to call him twice and he rejected my call both times. He's literally never done that," I explain.

"Well, fuck him," Clay says. "Let's go grab some food and we can go to the office."

"Food sounds amazing," I remark.

"I already ate, but I could probably eat again," Cam says casually. A blush heats my cheeks that I can't hide with Clay looking at me. He narrows his eyes at me and I fold.

"Stop it," I complain.

"Stop what?" Clay asks simply.

"Staring at me."

"Sorry, can't help it," he smiles.

"Can we go?" I ask impatiently.

"Go on," he laughs. When I step past him, he pokes me in the side, making me squeal and jump away.

"Now I remember why I hated when you three were together," I say. Clay moved here when he was seventeen, but they were pretty close. They still are, just from a distance. It makes me curious if they trust him enough to know about me and Cam. I assume so, considering Cam made a joke about it, knowing I could react that way.

Chapter Twenty-Two
Lorelei

WE ARE SITTING AT the large conference room table, and I am focused on my laptop as I type. We finished one meeting, and the next will start after a while. Hands start massaging my neck and I groan as I drop my head and relax. I notice right away that it's Clay, but I don't stop him.

"Feel good?" Clay chuckles.

"Sounds like it does," Cam remarks.

"Bite me, Cam," I sigh. I gasp and jump up when he actually stands and advances on me.

"What's wrong?" Cam asks with a grin.

"Psycho," I say. He narrows his eyes and backs me into a corner. "Cam. Cameron. There's..."

Cam grabs my face and kisses me, and I can't help but melt. When he pulls away, I smack his arm. "We told him, Lori," Cam says. "Cute seeing you blush, though."

"I'm uncomfortable," I laugh nervously.

"You're going to be more uncomfortable if you smart off to me again," Cam warns.

"That's one way to get your sister to stop being a brat," Clay laughs. "Just fuck her real good."

"Don't feed into their psychosis, Clay. You'll end up just like them," I say.

"Sounds like if being like them will land me inside you. I think I'll take that chance," he says coolly. Cam laughs and hugs me when my face flushes again.

"Imagine that. Little Lori with three cocks stuffed in her," Cam whispers in my ear.

"Cam," I sigh.

"Just think about it," he says quietly. "Remy and I talked, and he's wanted to fuck you for years. We both want to see him fuck you."

"Cam," I say as I pull away.

"Yes?" He grins.

"Really?"

"Yep. Oh... We are staying at his house," Cam says. I sigh heavily, and Clay laughs.

"Jesus," I sigh. "Whatever. The next meeting is starting."

"Oh, don't be like that," Cam says.

"Like what? Like someone who is sick of finding out everything last?" I snap. "Like someone who is scared of *more* people dying because someone wants to hurt me?"

People start coming into the room, and Cam backs off to let me sit back with my laptop. As they get started, I focus on taking notes. The meeting is with Clay and his board members, so I don't really know why we are here. I don't know what to take notes on, so I note everything. Every word. Every joke. It keeps my mind off things, and I am thankful for that. When the meeting is over but everyone is still chatting, I see a message from Dad pop up on my laptop.

Dad

> Hey, kid. See you are online.

> Hey! Yeah. You have internet?

> Yeah. I got Wi-Fi up here so we could reach out to people. How's Florida?

> We are actually in Seattle. Little switch-a-roo

Ah! Sneaky. They know who tried to kill you?

> No one has said, but I think it was a friend of mine from the club. He was supposed to go up and sit with you and Mom, but kinda disappeared. It's the only thing that makes sense. I don't know why he'd want to shoot me, though.

He? Rob?

> No. Omar.

Ah. Well, maybe not. He could have just decided to leave.

> Maybe. How's Mom?

She's good. Watching her shows.

> Sounds about right! Meeting is over so I've got to go. I love you, Dad!

Love you too, kid. Be safe.

"Everything okay?" Cam asks. I look up and see that it's just Clay, Cam, and Remy in the room now.

"Huh? Oh. Yeah, I'm okay. I was chatting with Dad. They have Wi-Fi now apparently," I say.

"No, they don't," Cam says.

"Well, he was messaging me, so they must have it now," I shrug. "Why are you all staring at me?"

"I'm sorry that we didn't talk to you before we made decisions," Cam says carefully.

"No, don't be," I sigh. "I shouldn't have snapped. I'm just... I don't get why Omar would want to kill me not too long after hugging me and telling me he was sorry about Tris drying. Could someone be that evil?"

"Yeah," Clay says. "They'd have to be completely devoid of emotion. They wouldn't know what it is, but they could mimic it to manipulate others."

"I just wish I knew what Tris was thinking before she died," I sigh.

"That would make investigations too easy if you knew exactly what they were thinking," Clay chuckles. "Let's grab dinner and go to the house."

"Why are we staying with you?" I ask bluntly when we stand.

"Because I have a ten-foot privacy wall and an equally tall iron fence," Clay says. "My property is the safest place for you... Despite what Cameron is making it out to be, this is primarily for your safety."

"Oh," I say. "I am guessing Cam is accurate to some degree, though?"

"Do you want him to be?" Clay asks, raising an eyebrow at me. My cheeks flush again, and he smiles. "I'll take that as your answer."

"Why exactly did we sit in on your board meeting?" I ask, changing gears.

"We've been considering partnering with Holden Technology for a while now. We wanted to get a feel for everything. I thought you knew this?" Cam asks.

"I... You know, I think that was mentioned. I guess I just didn't connect it," I say. "Well, I took notes of... well, everything. I'll condense it down to not every single spoken word later."

"Let's go get something to eat," Clay says.

"Oh, I could definitely eat again," Cam says, looking me up and down. When my cheeks flush and he chuckles, I punch him in the arm.

"Ow! Brat!" he laughs as he rubs his arm.

"Knock it off." I frown.

"Teasing you is so much fun, though," he says.

"Mhmm. Let's go," I sigh.

Chapter Twenty-Three
Lorelei

When we walk into Clay's home, it is welcoming. He has a large plush sectional and a huge ottoman. The décor is simple, but elegant. Overall, it is gorgeous. "Kitchen is to the left. Down the hall is my office and a guest bathroom. Upstairs has the master bedroom and guest rooms," Clay says.

"You have a beautiful home," I say.

"Thank you," he says.

"Are we going anywhere else?" I ask Remy.

"No. Go change. I know you want to," he laughs.

"I'll show you the bedrooms," Clay says, waving me to come along. I trail behind him while Remy and Cam follow with the bags. When we get down the hall, Clay takes us into a room that looks like the master bedroom.

"Is this your room?" I ask.

"It is," he says. I stop walking and everyone looks at me. "Come here."

"Why?" I ask skeptically. He chuckles and walks over to grab my hand. I let him lead me to the bathroom door where he points to a massive jacuzzi.

"Thought you'd want to relax," he says.

"Oh, hell. Okay," I say, and he chuckles.

"Hey, Lori. Want some tea?" Remy asks, wiggling his eyebrows at me.

"So, I can drown in the bath for real this time? No, I think I'll pass." I say.

"I'll get it started. You can relax and get out of your head for a while," he says.

"Thank you, Clay," I say sweetly.

"You are welcome, Lori," he says. He starts filling the huge tub and I turn to the bags.

"Are we crossing a boundary?" Remy asks, turning me to face him.

"No," I say simply.

"Why do you seem upset, then?"

"I'm just... he just makes me nervous is all," I say.

"How?" Cam asks.

"I don't know. Just his energy, I guess," I say, assuming Clay cannot hear me as I speak softly.

"What do you mean?" Cam asks.

"It's like... He just seems a lot more dominant," I say. "Like I would be far less likely to get away with being a brat."

"Little brats who misbehave get punished," Clay says softly in my ear. "Want to find out how?"

Remy and Cam smile but say nothing. "No," I squeak out.

"Aww. No?" he asks. "You had so much to say earlier... Actually... You were snapping instead of communicating."

"Oh, fuck you, Clay," I start to say. This man snatches me by my throat and pulls me up to my tiptoes so fast that I think I stop breathing for a second. Clay is a big man with this energy about him that exudes dominance.

"Excuse me?" he asks with a dangerous tone. "You are going to learn very quickly that I will not tolerate attitude. They may go easy on you, but I will not. If you need something, open that pretty little mouth and ask. Is that understood?"

"Yes," I whisper.

"I'm sorry?" he asks. When I don't say it, he tightens his grip on my throat.

"Yes sir," I choke out. He releases me but tips my chin up.

"Now, go take a bath and relax," he says. "Do you need anything?"

"No," I whisper. He narrows his eyes and fucking growls at me. It instantly makes my knees weak and I correct myself. "No sir!"

"Good girl. Go on," he says sweetly.

Just like that... They all walk out. What the fuck just happened? I stand in the middle of the room, still in shock. It takes me a few seconds before I go into the bathroom and shut the water off. Once I strip down, I step into the hot, bubbly water and sit in the far back corner. I lay my head back and try to pretend there isn't a third man in this house I want to fuck. What the fuck is wrong with me? Eh, fuck it. Worst case, I can kill myself, so I never have to worry about getting judged. That is definitely an intrusive thought that should stay inside my head.

I hear someone come in, but I don't say anything. The bubbles conceal me, but it doesn't matter one bit when I can sense they are all here and undressing. After a second, I open my eyes to find all three of them naked and getting in the water with me. My eyes go wide when I see Clay, but I snap them shut and pretend that I did not just see that he has a monster cock that legitimately scares me. Remy and Cam are big, but Clay? Deadly.

"What was that?" Remy asks.

"Hmm?" I ask. "Nothing. Nope. I'm good."

"Are you lying?" Clay asks.

"No," I say. I can feel my face burning with my lie, so I give myself up. "Fine. Yes. I am."

"What was that look for, then?" Cam asks.

"Why do you all have to have giant dicks?" I ask, opening my eyes. "I thought you and Remy were big, but goddamn. Here is Clay, over here with a fucking monster in his pants. How the fuck do you walk? Do you just pick a pant leg?"

"You are so dramatic," Clay laughs.

"Pick a number between one and three," Remy says.

"What? Why?" I ask.

"Pick."

"One," I say. "Higher numbers sound scary."

"You choose Clay," Cam says with a smile.

"For what? What is going on?"

"It means they will fuck you together, but I will get you alone," Clay says.

"Can I... opt for all?" I ask, making them all look at me in surprise. "But I get to decide who is where?"

"Why?" Remy asks with a smirk,

"Why not?"

"Okay," Clay says. "But, you give up your safe word."

"Why?" I ask.

"Why not?" He smiles wickedly, and I know I'm in trouble.

"Okay. No safe word," I agree.

"Who do you want to ride?" he asks.

"You."

"Taking your ass?"

"Remy."

"And Cameron throat fucks you," he confirms, and I nod. "Come here."

"No," I say without thinking

"Actually," he says. "Dry off and go sit on the bed."

"What happened to relaxing?" I ask.

"What happened to not having an attitude?" he asks. "You forfeited your safe word. Go, or I'll move you myself. If I have to do that, you'll be punished."

"Yeah. Okay," I laugh, feeling brave. It's when they all stand that I know I have truly fucked up. Cameron reaches for me first, and when I move away from him, I scream out as Clay grabs me by the hair and pulls me out of the tub. "Wait. Wait... Clay!"

He abruptly turns me around and shoves my face down into the water. He starts smacking my ass over and over again. He doesn't stop until everything starts to darken, and then pulls me up. I gasp for air and cough, but try to calm myself when he grabs me by the throat and pulls me close. Remy dries my body as Clay stares me down. When he is done, Clay finally speaks.

"Go sit on the bed," he growls.

"Yes sir," I whisper. When he releases me, I turn and glare at both Remy and Cam before walking past them to the room. Before I have the chance to sit, he comes out of nowhere and smacks my ass again. This time, I turn and try to shove him away. He growls and grabs my wrist before twisting it behind my back and shoving me over the bed. They all work together as I thrash around to tie my arms behind my back. I am left on the bed for a moment, but I hear them doing something close by.

I am pulled up to my feet and turned to face a bench of sorts. It has a spot where you straddle it, only it has your legs far enough apart that everything is exposed. Clay shoves me forward and Remy picks me up to sit me on it so I am sitting comfortably. I am on my knees, but my legs are very far apart. It almost forces me into a sitting position to be comfortable. My arms are attached to it so that I can move forward, but then Cam puts a collar around my neck that attaches to a hook on the front. I am completely restrained once they put straps around my thighs to make sure I cannot move my legs.

I say nothing because I want to know what they are doing, but I also don't want to make it worse and get myself in more trouble.

"Open your mouth," Clay says. I do, and he shoves a ball gag in my mouth before tying it around my head. A blindfold covers my eyes and headphones are placed over my ears, leaving me without the sense to hear, see, speak or the ability to move. Someone spreads lube all over my pussy and ass before fingers start working it into me. When they move away, two long, thick dildos are pushed into my pussy and ass. I groan and whimper as I am filled, but it's the wand being pressed against my clit that catches my attention.

"One hour," Clay says in my ear when he lifts up for a moment. They are playing simple white noise. The dildos start to move, and I try to move away from it. I scream around the gag when a sudden zap shocks my back. Did they just use a stun gun on me? The dildos alternate, so one is always pushing into me. Their speed and depth increase. When the wand comes to life, the vibrations make me scream. Everything seems to all come up at once and the dildos starts fucking me impossibly fast and hard. They are so goddamn deep that it almost hurts. My only saving grace is the wand that is making me come back-to-back.

One fucking hour. Those motherfuckers left me on this goddamn devil machine for an hour. I know this, because every fucking minute that passes, a robotic voice tells me how many minutes are left. I can tell that they are reapplying lube because suddenly everything is smoother, and my moans come easier. I enter into almost like a meditative state. I am drooling all over my neck and chest from having this ball gag in. I am a hot fucking mess, but they stay with me the entire time. One of them is always rubbing my shoulders, gently rubbing their hand up and down my thigh, or another gentle gesture to let me know they have not left me.

When the voice tells me the time is up, I am pulled off the bench and everything is taken off me. I am hardly able to stand, so Clay grabs the backs of my thighs and moves to sit on the bed. You'd think I'd be ready to take him after all that, but no. He slams me down on his cock and a scream rips from my throat. When he lays back, he brings me with him so he can lift his hips and start fucking me hard and fast.

"Fuck! Too hard. Oh, my God. Please," I whimper. He starts thrusting even harder and I beg him to stop. "Please. Stop. Please. It hurts. Clay!"

Remy grabs my hips and slams into my ass seconds before Cam grabs my face and shoves his cock down my throat. He matches their pace and they all brutally fuck me with absolutely no regard for my comfort.

The thing is... this is what I've been missing. This brutality is what I have needed to truly open myself up and accept that I cannot control everything. Giving up this control feels like freedom; it's the sweetest fucking pain I have every felt and I'll want it again. And again. And again.

I am sucking Cameron's dick like my life depends on it, making him come first. Remy and Clay sit me up and Remy wraps his hands around my throat. When he tightens his grip and I cannot breathe, I know what his goal is. I relax into the idea that I will soon be unconscious. As the world starts to fade, the most explosive orgasm splashes through my body and as my arousal floods out, I drag both men down into their own release.

Chapter Twenty-Four
Lorelei

I FEEL A HAND smacking my face and a voice coaxing me from my sleep. "Baby, you need to wake up... Lori... Come on... There you are... open your eyes, baby," Remy says.

"Mmmm," I groan.

"I need you to wake up, love. We need to go," he says, pulling me up.

"Is she awake?" I hear Ross' voice ask.

"Yeah. We are packed up and ready to go," Cam says.

"What's going on?" I mutter. I see Ross and Andrea on Cam's phone as he brings it over to me. "Oh. Video chat. Hi."

"Omar is dead, Lori," Andrea says. Her words snap my brain awake in an instant.

"What?" I ask.

"Omar called 911 and talked with dispatch. He was saying he was going to kill himself, but he wanted to make sure you got a message," Ross says. "He said, 'You can't trust anyone. I didn't know who he was to you. I didn't know, I swear. I tried to shoot you. I didn't know what to do. Death is better than what he will do. Be sweet, Lolita. See you in the next life.' And then dispatch noted that a gunshot was heard and the line went silent. It remained silent until first responders found his body and the agent disconnected."

"Oh my God," I say. "I... Who killed Tris then?"

"I need you all to get on that plane and get back here as soon as possible. I don't trust anyone right now, so you need to come home. Okay?" Andrea says.

"Clay is coming with us," Remy says. "Everything is in his car."

"We will meet you at the airport," Ross says.

"You know who it is, don't you?" I ask.

"Yes, and I will tell you as soon as you get in that car and go," Ross says. "Please, go. Okay?"

"Okay," I say. I stand up and Remy hands me clothes to change into. I get dressed in record time and we rush out of the house and get into the car.

Once we are on the road, I turn back to Cam's phone. "Okay. We are driving toward the airport. Spill it," I say. I have Remy on one side of me and Cam on the other, so they can both see the phone.

Ross and Andrea look sad, almost pitiful. My mind starts to race, trying to think of someone else I would know, and the information is like a puzzle coming together in my head.

"No," I say when Ross opens his mouth to speak. "It can't..."

"What?" Cam asks.

"What are you thinking?" Andrea asks.

"It's Dad... isn't it?" I ask as tears roll down my cheeks.

"Yes," Andrea says in her usual blunt but soft tone.

"What? Dad? Are you sure?" Cam asks.

"Your DNA came back as a familial match to the semen sample left on and in Beatris' body, Cameron," Ross says. "Ted Belmont used to be Theodore Bianchi. He was the most prevalent mafia boss in New York but seemingly disappeared and went underground thirty years ago... Allison Belmont was a dancer at a club. We don't think that your mom is aware. We sent a unit to the cabin, and she was alone. She said that your father dropped her off and said that he was going to grab some supplies from a nearby store, but never returned. She was so far out that she couldn't really do anything, so she waited."

"So, she is safe?" I ask.

"Yes. She is in a safe-house but keeps trying to break out to go and kill your father. Rob is with her right now and that seems to be helping."

"Why me?" I ask. "Why do that to Tris?"

"Honestly… I don't know, Lorelei," Andrea says. "Now that we know it's him, we are easily connecting everything. Ted is connected to the three from the club that hurt you. He knows Omar because Omar owed the Bianchi family a lot of money in gambling debt. It seems like he was doing your dad's bidding, but when he realized at the funeral that you were his daughter, he flipped. I guess he thought killing you was more merciful than your dad getting to you."

"He was so… indifferent at the funeral," Cam says. "He's always sucked at showing emotion, but I thought he just bottled it up. He and Mom never fought… He was good to her… to us…"

"Uh…" I say. "I chatted with him… In the meeting…"

"Yeah," Cam says.

"I told him we were in Seattle," I say.

"Shit," Ross says. "Okay. Just get on the plane. We've informed Air Traffic Control and the pilot what is going on."

"We will be there in just a second," Clay says.

"Clay…"

"Nope. Don't try it," Clay says. "No fucking way I am sitting here while you are in danger."

"Clay, please..." I start to say.

"No, Lorelei. You can get mad, but you'll be mad with one other person looking after you," he says. "Pulling up."

"Almost to the jet," I tell Ross and Andrea.

"Okay. Be safe and stay on the plane until we get to you, okay?" Ross says.

"Okay. Thank you... for everything," I say. This feels like goodbye, so it seems appropriate to say my well wishes now.

"Come home, Lori," Ross says. "You can thank us when you are back in New York."

"Okay... See you later," I sigh. When the call ends, the car comes to a stop, and we all get out. I grab Tris' ashes, and the guys grab the bags. We get on the jet and store all of our bags while the pilot quickly goes through his checklist. We sit on the couches and try to be patient.

Several minutes pass before we finally start moving. "Poor Tris," I say. "She saw him as a father figure... She always did, even when her parents were alive."

"I can't imagine," Remy says. "And the fact she probably knew he meant to take you."

"He must have had help. I don't see him not knowing who I am," I say.

"Yeah, if he had a habit of making others do his dirty work, that is logical," Cam adds.

When we are in the air and the pilot turns the seatbelt light off, I get up to use the restroom. Before I go back to the others, I take a second to look at myself I the mirror. I haven't really seen myself in a long time, but I do right now. I look worn down and exhausted; more so than usual. I can't wait to put all of this behind us.

I step out of the bathroom and a hand immediately covers my mouth. When I feel the barrel of a gun press to my temple, dread washes over me. "Walk," Dad says simply. I listen and take a few steps down the small hallway. Cam is the first to look up and rage fills his eyes.

"Dad, let her go," Cam booms as they all stand.

"Sit on the couch. All together," Dad says. His voice is even and calm, which is the scariest part. "If I have to repeat myself, I will blow her brains out. Go."

Reluctantly, they all sit on the couch. He keeps his attention on them as he places handcuffs on my wrists behind my back. He pushes me down to sit on the couch opposite of them, before going over and restraining them with zip ties. Once he has their lap belts on and tight, he turns to me.

"Daddy, please stop," I say tearfully. "Why are you doing this?"

"Because I can," he says simply. "The plan was for me to sell you off, but Beatris never spoke up and told my men they grabbed the wrong person. That fucked it all up, so here we are."

He stands and goes back toward the back. When he returns, he has a large butcher's knife in hand. It still has dried blood on the blade and fear washes over me. "Dad, stop this. She is your daughter."

Dad rolls his eyes and grabs tape. One by one, he cuts off a piece and places it over their mouths. "Now... Where was I... Oh, yes... Tris lasted longer than I thought. I didn't think she'd stay conscious until the end. She stayed just as tight long after she stopped breathing, even being cut open like she was."

"You are sick," I scream at him. He suddenly slaps me across the face, and it stuns me. He has never hit me or even raised his voice when he got mad. How is this the same gentle man who raised us?

Dad lays me down on my back with my arms still cuffed behind me. I fight back sobs as he starts cutting my clothing off. "Such a beautiful body, Lori. Just like your mother," he remarks as he cuts my bra off. I look over at Cam, Remy, and Clay, and they are all crying. Rage is still burning in their eyes, but they are helpless. All they can do is watch and pray he doesn't do to me what he did to Tris.

"Daddy, please don't," I whimper.

"Mmm. Tris didn't beg, but I bet you will," he says with a smile as he looks over my now naked body. "You and I have six hours together. How should we spend it?"

"Please don't hurt me, Daddy," I cry. "Please."

"Let's see if we can get you to relax," he says as he pulls my legs apart.

"Stop! Please Don't..." I start to say but my words get stuck in my throat when he brings the tip of the knife to graze along my inner thigh. He is just inches from my pussy, and I am so goddamn scared right now.

"You fight me, and I'll cut your clit off," he warns. "The screams that women make when it's sliced off... Please, fight me. I am already so fucking hard thinking about it."

I nod and choke back my sobs, trying to regain control of my emotions. Dad grabs lube out of the bag he brought in with the knife and coats his fingers. He pushes three fingers into me and I squeeze my eyes shut. I feel his hot breath on me before slowing licking across my clit. "Oh, Pumpkin. You taste just like your mom," Dad rumbles. He starts to move his fingers inside of me as his tongue swirls and flicks my clit. I am panting, trying so hard to not let it break me. I instantly break when he sucks hard.

"Fuck!" I moan. He sucks harder and starts fucking me with his hand. Within seconds, it breaks, and I come so hard that my ears ring. I instantly start sobbing and he chuckles as he pulls me up and moves me over to stand in front of Cam. He unlocks my cuffs and pushes me forward.

"Show your brother what a good girl you are for daddy," he says. "Bend over and suck your brother's cock."

"Dad," I start to say but whimper in pain when he smacks me on the side of the head.

"Now. Bend and suck, Lorelei," he says.

I sigh and lean over to unbutton his jeans. I go slowly so I don't give away the truth about Cameron and me. I keep eye contact with him as I pull his dick out. He isn't hard, but the second I touch him, he starts to harden in my hand. I lazily stroke him as my dad keeps his hands on my hips. I glance over at Remy and mouth the question, "Is he going to do it?" Remy nods ever so slightly, which tells me that my dad is about to rape me.

I take a deep breath and wrap my lips around Cameron's cock. Dad immediately lines himself up and slams into me, making me wince. I focus on Cameron and suck hard as I bob up and down, trying to ignore that my father is pounding into me. I realize that I am not on birth control, and this man is about to come in me. If I get knocked up by my own father, I'll throw myself into traffic.

"Fuuuck," Dad groans. He abruptly pulls out of me and away from Cameron. His dick is still hard as Dad shoves me to the ground. The knife is close, but not in his hands, so I choose to fight. When he straddles my body, I bring my knee up to hit him in the dick. He screams out in pain when an audible popping sound is heard. He goes to grab the knife, but I bring my leg up and kick him in the chest. It stuns him enough that I can get my legs around his throat and lock my ankles. He is hitting my legs and trying to breathe, but I don't let go. I am screaming as I go through the realization that I am killing my father. Yesterday, I never imagined that Dad could hurt anyone. Right now, he is a fucking monster who doesn't deserve to breathe.

I am screaming at him, cursing him for taking my best friend. At some point, the copilot comes out to find what's happening. He unties the guys and it's Cameron who gets me to stop.

"He's gone, Lori. Baby, he's gone. It's okay," he says as he gently coaxes me into releasing him. When I do, he wraps me in a blanket and scoops me up so he can hold me in his lap. I am sobbing hysterically, grieving my father. I trusted him. As a little girl, he promised me once that he would always protect me from the monsters, but he became one instead. In one day, I find closure for Tris and lose my dad.

Eventually, I fall asleep in Cameron's lap, only to be woken by Ross' voice. "Lorelei," he says softly. My eyes snap open, and he smiles softly.

"He hurt me," I whimper.

"Yeah, but it looks like you got him back," he smirks. I sit up in Cameron's lap and he hugs me tightly. This has nothing to do with our love and everything to do with us losing our father, or the monster who pretended to be our father.

"I killed him," I say. "Am I in trouble?"

"You also broke his dick," Andrea says. "And no. You are not in trouble. The jet has a camera."

"Just out here, right?" I ask, and Cameron laughs.

"Not in the bedroom," Clay says as he pulls me up. He hugs me tightly and kisses my temple before Remy gets me. Remy kisses me before scooping me up to take me off the plane.

"Don't forget Tris!" I say.

"I got her," Cameron laughs.

"How did I break his dick?" I ask.

"You kneed the shit out of him," Remy says. "Did you not hear it?"

"I was just focused on him not getting that knife."

Remy carries me off the plane and the place is swarming with cops. We get into Andrea's SUV, and I stay in Remy's arms. Clay and Cam get in with us and I stretch my legs across their lap as I lay my head on his chest.

"I love you, guys," I say.

"We love you too," Remy says, kissing the top of my head.

"Aww. Me too?" Clay asks teasingly.

"It's new, but I want you in my life permanently," I say honestly.

"We have a lot to talk about, but a lot to settle first," Cam says.

"The media will love this," I say, rolling my eyes.

"We already released that it was Ted," Andrea says. "You all shouldn't have to deal with the media much. They might bother you for a few days, but they'll move on."

"I just want to go home and sleep," I say as I close my eyes. "Super glad I didn't get nutted in by my father."

"You're so crude," Remy laughs.

"It's trauma, baby," I sing, but break out into laughter.

Chapter Twenty-Five
Lorelei

MY EYES FLUTTER OPEN and I gasp when I see Clay's face inches from mine. "Morning," he says with a grin. I frown deeply at him and he kisses the tip of my nose.

"I don't wanna be awake," I mutter.

"Well, you've been asleep since yesterday when we were in the car, so... you have to get up," he says, smacking my ass.

"Ow! Asshole," I say but squeal when he grabs my ankles and drags me to the end of the bed. I laugh when he nearly pulls me off the bed, but I manage to stand. "You're persistent."

"You need to eat," he says.

"Where are Cameron and Remington?" I ask as I go to the dresser and get a pair of leggings to put on.

"Making breakfast. Andrea and Ross are here. Your mom, I believe, should be here too," he says, watching me get dressed.

"Ah," I say. "Well, alright."

We go downstairs and everyone turns and smiles at me. "Hey," I say with a sigh.

"Hey, sweetheart," Mom says as she hugs me.

"Hey, Momma," I mutter.

"I am so sorry he hurt you, baby," she says. "I had no idea. I don't even know what to say."

"Well, he's dead now, so it's whatever," I say. "What's for breakfast?"

"French toast," Cam says. I nod and sit at the table.

"What are we doing today?" I ask, looking at Ross.

"I think it would be wise for you to make a statement," Ross says.

"Okay."

"Are you okay?" Andrea asks.

"Yep. Anything else?"

"No," she says slowly. Everyone is looking at me and it's pissing me off.

"Okay. Well, I will make a statement but I'm going to the office. I have some things…"

"Lori, no," Remy says with a frown.

"I wasn't asking for permission, Remington," I snap. "I'll grab something to eat on the way."

I stand and find my purse before walking to the door. "Lori, you can't be off by yourself," Cam says as everyone follows me.

"Why?" I ask, yelling at him. "He's dead, Cameron. I did that. The problem is solved, so I'm going to work. Sit here and pout if you want."

I turn and walk out of the house and go to my car. I haven't driven in a while and it feels nice to be alone finally. I get in and lock the door before anyone can get to me. When I get to the gate, it won't open right away. When I put it in reverse with a plan to break the fucker down, it opens.

I turn the music up loud and just drive. There is a part of me that wants to keep going and never look back. If I just run away, everyone could be rid of me. All I have done is bring chaos. I killed my mother's husband, my brother's father, my father... I killed him to save myself. To avenge Beatris. I did it without thinking or hesitating. What kind of monster does that make me? What fucks me up the most is that I don't regret it. I don't feel bad. I don't care that he's gone. The part of me that just wanted my daddy back, the man who raised me, that part is gone and I'm glad the bastard is dead. I just wish he could've suffered the way Tris did.

When I pull into the parking lot, the reporters spot me getting out of the car immediately. I know everyone else will be close behind me, but it's definitely a statement for me to show up alone.

"Lorelei! What do you have to say about your father?" someone shouts at me. I turn and face them as I see everyone pull into the lot next to my car.

"The man who raised me is gone. He was gone long before he hurt my best friend, long before he snuck onto that plane and hurt me. That man never existed and the monster that he really was created this façade of a loving husband, father, friend, boss, and so much more. He manipulated and tricked everyone around him into believing that he was a good person. My thoughts are simple; I'm glad he's dead, but I wish he had suffered."

A turn and walk into the building and go straight to the elevator. I have every intention of locking myself in my office. I don't care if I have to barricade the door, I just want to work and everyone leave me the fuck alone. As the elevator door closes, I see everyone rushing to the elevator to get to me. About halfway up the building, I pull the emergency stop. They can't get to me if I've locked myself in here.

I slide down the wall to sit on the floor and tears roll down my cheeks. My phone starts to ring in my purse, and I reluctantly get it out to answer. "What?" I sniffle.

"Where are you, Lorelei?" Cameron asks.

"In the elevator," I say, my voice breaking.

"Start it back up and come talk to me, please. Just me and you, okay?"

"I killed him," I whimper.

"I know, sweetheart. Start it back and let me get to you. Okay?"

"Okay," I say after a few seconds. I stand up and start the elevator. It immediately opens on the next floor and I see everyone standing there waiting. As promised, only Cameron gets in. When the doors shut, Cameron scans his badge and takes us to the basement.

When it opens up, Cam takes my hand and leads me out. The basement is primarily used for storage, but there is also an office area down here. "Why are we here?" I ask.

"Because no one will look for us down here," he says. "Remy is the only other one with access."

"Okay," I say simply. We get into the back office and he locks the door before walking over to me. "What are you doing?"

"Whatever I want," he says as he yanks my leggings down. I kick off my shoes and step out so he can pick me up. He has my legs draped over his arms as he grips onto me. I unbutton his jeans to pull his cock out, and he slams into me.

"Fuck," I gasp.

"Who am I, Lorelei?" he asks.

"Cameron," I say as he slowly fucks me but stays deeps. "My brother."

"Do you regret letting me inside you?"

"No," I pant. "God, I love it. I love you."

"Good girl," he praises. "I love you so fucking much, Lori. I will love you no matter who you kill, why you did it, who is next, or if you regret it. We are not judging you. Not even the media is. You did what you had to do, and now he is dead."

"I'm glad he's dead," I say.

"So am I. I am also glad you like my cock so much." He smirks. "Do you understand the point here?"

"No," I sigh and lean my head back.

"Our family is seriously fucked up," he says. "Incest, crime, trafficking, assault, drugs, and everything else in between. So, now we have another murder to add to the mix. So what? I don't care, Bloomington doesn't care, the cops don't care, Clay still wants to fuck you stupid, and we will all be okay."

"Mom cares," I groan.

"Don't talk about our mother when my cock is buried inside of you," he laughs.

"Then fuck me and stop messing around," I frown. He grins mischievously before standing me up. He turns me around and lays me across the desk before slamming back into me. This time he starts fucking me hard and fast, pushing as deep as he can. I cover my mouth and moan wildly as he fucks me like it's a race. It feels so goddamn good to have him this deep. He grabs me by the hair and pulls my head back, which makes me put my hands on the desk for support. He resumes covering my mouth for me and goes harder. My eyes are rolled back into my head as he pounds into me, and the huge oak desk creaks with every thrust. It sounds like it's going to fall apart, but not if I do first.

"You're such a fucking slut for me, aren't you?" he growls.

"Mhmm," I whimper into his hand.

"Come for me, Lori. Show your big brother just how much of a fucking whore you are... Fuck, you feel so goddamn good... so tight..."

When my orgasm crashes over me, his drags us further down. When he pulls out of me, he lifts me up and lays me across the desk. I immediately have to slap my hand over my face as he dives in and starts eating his come out of my pussy. He pushes his tongue into me and is practically drinking from my body. I am desperately rocking my hips, wanting more. When he latches on and starts sucking my clit, I scream into my hand. I grabbed the back of his head and start grinding my pussy against his mouth. My movement causes him to tug and pull at my clit, but it's when his teeth bite down on me that everything explodes again.

"Oh my God," I say breathlessly when he helps me put my leggings back on. "Christ, Cameron."

"Like that?" he asks with a grin. "Figured it would be best if my come wasn't leaking out of you when we returned to the others. I suspect that might give us away."

"You... are crazy," I say. He captures my mouth and kisses me hard, making me relax.

"Now, what about Mom?"

"Why isn't she upset about Dad?" I ask. "She's just as indifferent as he was. I didn't see it until Dad, but they're both like that."

"Yeah," he sighs. "Andrea and Ross are still investigating her, but... I don't trust it. Dad accidentally ended up with Tris and brutally murdered her. He knew he was going on that plane and would end up dying. That was a suicide mission. He would've killed Mom, not left her there at the cabin."

"What if she was actually running things?" I ask.

"We could take a risk and corner her. Make her think we know and see if she cracks," Cam suggests.

"Worst-case scenario, she thinks we are crazy," I shrug.

"Baby, we are crazy," he laughs before kissing me again. "Next time, just talk to us. Okay?"

"Okay. I'm sorry I was a bitch. I was spiraling," I say.

"Yeah, I figured. Your night terrors were intense," he says. "Let's go back up. I have an idea on how to corner her."

Chapter Twenty-Six
Lorelei

"Are you absolutely sure about this?" I ask Cameron. "What if we are wrong?"

"We blame it on trauma," he shrugs. "Wanted to know. Now we know."

"And if we are right?"

"Andrea and Ross are listening and recording. They'll catch it all," he says.

"Okay," I sigh.

We are in the office on the first floor. No one else is here, but we asked Mom to come over and discuss Dad and his funeral arrangements. We aren't claiming his body, but that's not important. She is going to walk in on Cameron and me kissing and go from there.

Ross got her DNA from a cup she used at the police station and it came back as a familial match to Dad as a cousin and our mother.

We would only know this if we know that she is also living under a fake name. She will only mention it if she is giving herself up. Also, she knows that we are alone, so if she wants to kill me, now's the chance.

I am leaning back against the desk and Cameron is standing in front of me with his hands on the desk. He is close and I smile up at him. "She's in the house," he says before gently kissing me. I bring my hands to his face and we get swept away in our kiss. We hear her footsteps, but pretend we don't. When the door opens, silence. It takes us a few seconds before we pull apart. Cameron immediately pulls me behind him and I catch a glimpse of Mom holding a gun.

"Mom," Cam says carefully. "Put the gun down."

"You know, guys. I should have known you two would end up together," she says as she walks into the room. "I let Theodore talk me into waiting to sell my skanky daughter, and look where we are now? Brother and sister..."

"Mom," I say. "You are scaring me."

"You are scaring me," she mocks. "Shut the fuck up. You sound like your fucking father."

"Mom. What do you want?" Cameron asks calmly.

"Your sister," she says. "Give her to me and I won't blow your brains out."

"Then pull the trigger," Cameron says simply. He lifts the back of his shirt enough that I can see he has a gun in the waistband of his jeans. "I am not giving her to you, so aim well."

"Aww. How sweet of you to protect your little sister. Is she really worth dying for, though?" She asks. I hear her pull the hammer back and I take a deep breath before pulling the gun from its holster. I quietly and carefully check to make sure a round is chambered before getting a grip on it. The thing is, they can only hear us. We need her to admit to something because they can't see that she has the gun.

"Yes. You wouldn't have done that for Dad?" Cameron asks. "She is my family. You don't hurt family."

"Your father was a weak son of a bitch with a big ego and a short temper. He never should have killed Tris. I told that dumbass to get Lori on his own, but no. He wanted to have others do it for him. He realized he was cornered and what did he do? He went and got himself killed. The dumb fucker stranded me out there, even though we were safe. No one would have suspected shit," she says. "Now, I have you two idiots thinking you can trick me so the cops can come in and arrest me. Well, newsflash. I'm not going to jail. So, kiss your sister goodbye, because we are all dying here today. Our family line will end and everything I've worked for will disappear... all because your dumbass father just *had* to go and stick his dick in Beatris and leave his DNA behind."

"Momma," I say with a meek voice as I peek out from behind Cameron.

"What, Lorelei?" Mom snaps.

"Please, put the gun down," I ask, keeping my voice small.

"Oh, fuck you, Lor..." The second she raises the gun to shoot me, I pull the pistol out from behind Cameron and fire. The blast makes my ears ring and I am stunned.

One minute I am shooting my mother, and the next I am outside surrounded by people. There are voices and noises everywhere. Warm hands on my face center me, and I look up at Cameron. "I... She..." I choke out.

"She's gone, Lori. It's all over," he says as he hugs me. Remington sits beside me and wraps his arms around my body, only for Clay to join in and I am surrounded by them.

"It's over," I repeat back softly. Losing Tris and learning that my entire life was a lie should have collapsed my world, but these men are permanent structures in my life. Together, we carry the weight of the world, making each day easier than the last. We find strength in each other and peace when we need it the most. "Remy, thank you for helping me through this. Clay, you helped me find an escape from my mind, and I will always cherish that."

"We love you, Little Fawn," Remy says before softly kissing me.

I look to my brother with hopeful eyes and say, "Craving you shouldn't feel this good, but it does... Thank you for helping me find myself."

"You're welcome, sweetheart. Thank you for loving me," he says as he hugs me tightly. "Craving you saved us from ourselves."

Epilogue
Lorelei

Six Months Later

It's hard to believe that it's been six months since I lost my best friend and killed my parents. A lot has changed, but all for the better.

Sam has taken over as COO at the location in New York City. We merged with Holden Technology and rebranded everything with Saltz-Holden Technologies. By publicly denouncing the Belmont name, it saved us a fuck ton of backlash. We spent weeks flying back and forth to settle everything, but we got it worked out.

With Mom and Dad dying, it meant that Cameron and I inherited everything of theirs. We decided to liquidate everything, take the life insurance money, and put it all into a nonprofit. We named it the Beatris Cooper Foundation. We help survivors of sexual assault, human trafficking, domestic violence, and violent crimes with whatever they need. We also offer the families of victims that did not survive help by paying for funeral costs, and whatever they may need. Sometimes the victims have children or a spouse that depended on them and their income, so helping financially takes a burden off them so they can grieve. Three months ago, this foundation went live and we have since raised close to ten million dollars.

I wish Tris was here to see all the good that has come of her death. She was a very humble woman, but even this would make her feel special. She went through something horrific that ultimately led to my survival. I am not a religious person, but I thank God for her every day, but I pray I get to see her again someday.

We spread some of Tris' ashes in New York, a little bit was thrown into the Pacific Ocean, and then I made five necklaces. One for me, Cameron, Remington, Clay, and our unborn daughter. Three months ago, on the morning of the foundation launch, I found out I was eight weeks pregnant. I am now five months pregnant with a little girl and I simply couldn't be happier. Obviously, we know that Cameron isn't the father, but he will be considered a dad just as much as Remington or Clay. We don't talk about being biological siblings, and no one asks. Sam is aware of the situation, but I don't think anyone is willing to ask any questions. We know that Remington is the biological father of our baby, because we paid attention to ovulation windows. This will be confirmed at birth for the sake of genetics, but I am legally married to Remington, so I could take his last name.

Clay's mother had the idea for her to do an adult adoption and legally make Remington and Cameron her sons. This meant that Cameron could change his last name to Holden. It doesn't change genetics, but it makes it appear that he is my brother-in-law, not my actual brother. In all honestly, I don't care. I know it is illegal, but I'll take the risk. Cameron, Remington, and Clay are the loves of my life. If I have to hide my relationship with Cameron to keep us all together, I'll do it. If anyone finds out, oh well. We have enough saved and are confident it will not ruin what we've built.

Tris' urn with the remaining ashes sits in a case in the front lobby of the foundation. With it is her picture and a photo we took of her, me, Cameron, and Remington, a few months before she died. We have a table set up with a notepad and a lockbox. The sign simply says, "Letters to Tris." This is meant for people to be able to vent, complain, give good news, or say whatever they want to say to Tris. No one reads them, and I burn them all every few days. We have a version online, only it is sent to an email that automatically deletes it. I have the password for the email, but just like with the written letters, I don't read them. I write a letter to Tris every week and burn it with the others. Cameron does as well, and I think it's helping him heal. Tris was the kind of person that you could tell anything to, and she would never judge you. She might make a joke to make you smile, but she would always be open and accept you for who you are. I think finding a way for us to still talk to her in a way has allowed us to process things in a way we can't with anyone else.

I miss her so goddamn much that it hurts. I don't think it will ever stop hurting, but I am learning to live with the pain so that it doesn't suffocate me. As a way to honor her in a way that I know she would absolutely adore, we have decided to name our daughter Beatris Ann Saltz-Holden.

About the author

Dani Rose is a dark taboo pen name for the dark romance author, Emily Klepp. She is creating stories that make you question your morals and wonder why you chose to read taboo at all. Keeping separate from her usual trauma healing stories, this is the place where her intrusive thoughts run wild.

How to contact the author

https://linktr.ee/emilykleppnovels

www.ingramcontent.com/pod-product-compliance
Lightning Source LLC
LaVergne TN
LVHW041749060526
838201LV00046B/951